A
THOUSAND
WINGS

A THOUSAND WINGS

T. C. HUO

A DUTTON BOOK

DUTTON
Published by the Penguin Group
Penguin Putnam Inc., 375 Hudson Street, New York, New York 10014, U.S.A.
Penguin Books Ltd, 27 Wrights Lane, London W8 5TZ, England
Penguin Books Australia Ltd, Ringwood, Victoria, Australia
Penguin Books Canada Ltd, 10 Alcorn Avenue, Toronto, Ontario,
Canada M4V 3B2
Penguin Books (N.Z.) Ltd, 182–190 Wairau Road, Auckland 10, New Zealand

Penguin Books Ltd, Registered Offices:
Harmondsworth, Middlesex, England

First published by Dutton, an imprint of Dutton NAL,
a member of Penguin Putnam Inc.

First Printing, April, 1998
10   9   8   7   6   5   4   3   2   1

 REGISTERED TRADEMARK—MARCA REGISTRADA

Library of Congress Cataloging-in-Publication Data

Huo, T. C.
    A thousand wings / T. C. Huo.
       p.   cm.
    ISBN 0-525-94280-7
    I. Title.
    PS3558.U5314T48   1998
    813'.54—dc21   97-44987
                        CIP

Printed in the United States of America
Set in Fournier Tall Caps
Designed by Stanley S. Drate/Folio Graphics Co. Inc.

PUBLISHER'S NOTE
This is a work of fiction. Names, characters, places, and incidents either are the
products of the author's imagination or are used fictitiously, and any
resemblance to actual persons, living or dead, events, or locales is entirely
coincidental.

This book is printed on acid-free paper. ♾

ACKNOWLEDGMENTS

My thanks to the following, in chronological order of having contributed to this novel: Bertie Mo, David Silva, Eric Allyn, Mark Brack, Steve Kotz, for support and faith; Robert Pinsky, Thomas Keneally, for mentorship; the Nielsens, for a grant; Allyn Warrant, again, for support and faith; Marie Brown, my agent; and Rosemary Ahern, for inspiration.

A THOUSAND WINGS

"Salad is an integral part of eating egg roll. It provides a communal experience and lets you compose your own dish," Fong Mun told the guests as he stood at the head of the oval table.

The host of the dinner party, Fong Mun's accountant friend Tom, had asked him to show the guests how to serve egg rolls.

Fong Mun gave the demonstration only upon request, and kept it short, because experience had taught him that the guests would simply dive for the egg rolls with their forks or chopsticks, some with their hands, and altogether ignore the trays of red leaf lettuce, herbs, and rice noodles that also made up the dish.

He had put two pairs of tongs on each silver tray of greens, noodles, and egg rolls. Some of the golden brown egg rolls he had cut into bite-size sections with a pair of scissors. Half of the tray of egg rolls contained these small cubes; the other half, the full four-inch size.

He picked a leaf of the lettuce from the tray, put it squarely on his plate, and while fetching a sprig of cilantro and a sprig of large-leaf mint, said, "Add these as much as you like," and laid the cilantro and mint in the open leaf of lettuce.

The guests copied his motions, eyes watchful, hands both cautious and eager.

While he reached for the tray of noodles with a pair of chopsticks, Fong Mun happened to look up and caught a pair of eyes observing him at the far end of the table. Thick, inky eyebrows, eyes that spoke a lively, eloquent language, a sensuous mouth.

The pull of attraction, however, gave rise to a feeling of dejection. Over the years he had tried not to mind what the world would say about him. He knew it was more than his hair, his eyelashes, his face. People no longer mistook him (now at thirty-five) for a girl, as they had when he was a teenager, but some found evidence of effeminacy in his cookbook. The presentation of the recipes, his writing style, had a "delicate" feel, a "soft voice," according to reviewers and various readers who wrote to him.

None of Fong Mun's gay friends used such adjectives to describe him. And he hoped the stranger with the sensuous mouth wouldn't use such adjectives to describe him, either.

Fong Mun added a mouthful of rice noodles to the leaf of lettuce on the plate. Reaching for the tray of egg rolls, the chopsticks in his right hand, he glanced at the end of the table and back at the tray of food in front of him, and smiled. He put a bite-size segment of egg roll on top of the salad he had created and then folded the lettuce leaf into a pouch.

Here the guests fumbled. A piece of egg roll dropped from the chopsticks in a lawyer's shaky hand. He tried to recoup it, darting the chopsticks at the elusive piece of unyielding fried food. A poet who wrote experimental verse squeezed out the noodles and the mint from the leaf of lettuce on his plate, literally having taken Fong Mun's directions to "add these as much as you like" very much to heart.

Fong Mun regarded the bulgy leaf of lettuce in another guest's palm. "You have too much noodles and vegetables in there, Bill." The programmer looked up, wide-eyed like a child.

The experimental poet who, in his eagerness to eat, had made the mistake of taking Fong Mun's directions too literally, now managed to refold the leaf of lettuce into a pouch, but as he dipped it into a bowl of sauce, the pouch broke.

Watching the explosion of leafy pouches all around him, Fong Mun switched strategies. "Or we can mix everything on the plate," he said. "Easier that way." Again he took hold of a large leaf of lettuce, tore it to pieces, likewise the cilantro and mint. He then used a pair of chopsticks to transfer some rice noodles to his plate. He reached for the egg rolls next.

Usually, after the demo, he would leave and let the guests enjoy their meal. Sometimes he felt slightly sad upon leaving, unable to join the party. As he heard laughter and busy chatter, he reminded himself he was a caterer, a paid food provider. His presence at the party merely represented a commercial exchange. Increasingly, such transactions comprised his only contact with the world.

Fong Mun had told Tom, "If the guests rave about my food, it means this." He unfolded a news clipping—a review of his catering business—and quoted, " 'They appreciated the exquisite presentation, the complex and delicious flavors detonating in their mouths.' This joy, you see, is solipsistic by nature. Gratification and its opposite are nonshareable private experiences."

" 'Its opposite'?" Tom blinked.

Fong Mun folded the news clipping. "Hunger."

Rarely did appreciation extend to the person who provided those "complex flavors." Fong Mun therefore appreciated the e-mail messages his readers sent him. (Some women readers, kind and interested, inquired if he was married.)

"Of course I try to snap out of melancholy reflections," Fong Mun told Tom. "So while catering, I force myself to act cheerful, upbeat. While writing the cookbook, I fought a tendency to slip into a mournful tone, compelled to add as much spice to my prose as to the meals I serve."

But on cheerful occasions like the New Year, he would appear dejected or melancholy. On occasions that required him to show sadness or empathy—for example, at the news of Tom's father's death—he would feel lighthearted, jazzy. It was all askew.

Now, seated among the guests, Fong Mun glanced around the table; saw a few familiar faces; watched the guests, whose mouths took turns munching and then talking, talking and then munching, vigorous exercise for the jaw; took note of the young man who wore a deep blue sports jacket over a black crew-necked pull-over.

The lawyer who had dropped an egg roll proclaimed the importance of frying. Eyes turned to him. "What makes it taste so good?" He held a whole piece up. "It is not the wrapper, not the ingredients." He shook his head. "It's the frying. That's what's most vital. Bad frying ruins the crispy texture."

Smiling, Tom accorded Fong Mun a glance. Fong Mun returned it before he looked to the lawyer.

"How about the contents?" Bill, the programmer, asked as he slipped a piece into his mouth.

"Crispiness is vital. Contents become secondary," the lawyer pronounced.

"How about the filling? The seafood inside?" Bill pushed his point, his hand already on another firm piece of egg roll.

"All secondary. It's how the filling is packaged." The lawyer's one hand lingered along the length of the egg roll in his other hand, with the same care as he would handle an exhibit in court. "The golden brown, crunchy skin—this alone accounts for the quality. What distinguishes French fries is not the potato but the frying. Likewise, without its crunchy skin an egg roll fails."

Tom's smile deepened as the lawyer echoed his words: when Fong Mun first started out, Tom had used

French fries as an analogy to stress the importance of frying to Fong Mun.

Fong Mun told the lawyer it was the wrapper that accounted for the crispy texture he so loved. And how about the appetizing aroma that filled one's nose when biting an egg roll? How about the amount of black pepper in it? How about the jicama?

The experimental poet said the sauce alone accounted for the quality.

"The sauce?" Doubting his ears, Fong Mun looked to the poet. Then Fong Mun's eyes swept toward the stranger with the sensuous mouth and the pair of large, eloquent eyes.

The poet nodded emphatically. "It's so superb everything else becomes secondary."

"Including crunchiness?" The lawyer looked dismayed and incredulous.

The scrawny poet made a brush of his bony hand, to wave away the lawyer's claim, and went so far as to say that he could do without the egg roll altogether, but not the sauce.

All the others, including the stranger, watched this exchange go on.

Fong Mun turned to the poet and told him the sauce took the least time—and was the easiest—to make. Fong Mun's articulation—his voice growing full and rich—clearly was intended for someone other than the poet. Fong Mun's eyes shone with vital energy.

"Don't you care for crunchiness?" the lawyer addressed the poet.

While holding his bald lover's hand, the scrawny poet insisted adamantly on the supremacy of the sauce.

Fong Mun looked amused and was pleased to note a mild happiness in himself. With his emotions for once in their proper place, the timing for an auspicious event was right.

After dinner, the stranger sauntered over. He said he enjoyed the egg rolls. Did he enjoy the sauce too? Fong Mun asked. They laughed.

The conversation that followed revealed the stranger's name—Raymond. From Vientiane.

"Vientiane?" Fong Mun cried out. "I'm from Laos!"

This revelation also took Raymond by surprise.

"I don't remember anything about Laos. I left there when I was four," Raymond said.

Out of an impulse, a feeling both fraternal and maternal, Fong Mun reached out and brushed Raymond's soft black bangs aside. They moved closer.

"I've always wanted to know more about Laos," Raymond said.

"But you've heard adults talk, parents and relatives?"

"My father was missing—maybe captured by the comrades or the Thais. We don't know. My mother raised me." Raymond lowered his head. "I don't feel his absence." He raised his head. "I don't know what it feels like to have a father."

An urge to put his arm around Raymond, to pull him close—an urge akin to an ache, a mixture of sympathy and kindness and fondness—took hold of Fong Mun.

"For my mother it's different," Raymond continued. "She keeps her hope. She believes he's still alive."

"You're strong and healthy." And well-built. "Wherever he is, your father must be proud of you."

"I'm not so sure."

They drifted away, to chat with other guests, and drifted back again near the end of the party. Leaning on the kitchen counter, they stood side by side. Raymond asked for the recipe.

The request caught Fong Mun off guard. It struck him as too blunt, an affront. All along he had regarded the egg rolls as a secret pact between him and his grandmother. He had left the recipe out of his cookbook, kept it from readers, for fear they would tamper with it by substituting one ingredient for another.

Fong Mun groped for a way to voice his feelings. He had no real reason for withholding the recipe. To do so would be unreasonable and even selfish. He himself asked friends and relatives all the time for recipes when they cooked something he liked. Had he not taken poetic license, boldly modified the dish, and called the act creative? Did he not see recipes as dynamic, capable of evolving, open to reinvention?

Fong Mun told Raymond he never followed recipes strictly. "I approximate, mix and match. How much prawns to put? Depends. If I want to eat more prawns, I add more. I can do without the formulaic certainty a recipe provides."

Fong Mun's circuitous reply—neither a yes nor a no, but altogether an evasion—could be especially frustrating for a recipe seeker. The recipe still out of reach, Raymond half-protested, "Sure you don't need to measure the exact amount of ingredients—because you cook for a living. Sure it comes easy. You're a natural."

A natural? Fong Mun almost rushed to deny, but controlled himself. After all, he wanted to make a favorable impression. He smiled. "I can show you, from scratch."

They agreed on a date.

MORNING

On the morning of the following Saturday, a car drove up the wet inclined street in front of Fong Mun's condo on Potrero Hill. Dots of rain still remained on his front window, through which he saw the driver parking the car. The cloudy morning promised more rain.

After he ushered Raymond in, Fong Mun offered to show the cookbook he wrote, the catering brochures, and his Web site.

Of the three choices, Raymond responded with the most enthusiasm to the third. They looked at the garden on the computer screen: the garden in Sonoma County, north of San Francisco. "The vegetables you use are organically grown?"

"Yes." Fong Mun sat down next to Raymond.

"You grow them in your garden?"

"Some." Fong Mun leaned away from the screen. "I used to do gardening."

"You don't anymore?"

Fong Mun became thoughtful. "Not here. Not in California."

"But you have a garden. Look at this." Raymond pointed at the screen. "Isn't it yours?"

"The gardeners take care of it." One of the gardeners was Fong Mun's father, who lived on the premises, took care of the garden.

Raymond eyed Fong Mun.

"I'm too busy with the catering side of the business—I also cater wedding parties in the garden," Fong Mun said. "All one package." Fong Mun realized he had assumed his business persona. He chided himself for doing so, for talking to his date about—to use a Chinese expression—"firewood, rice, cooking oil, salt," the summation of his livelihood. Wouldn't he rather speak in a lover's tongue? But had he been more relaxed, he would have realized that Raymond was probably no stranger to the struggle for "firewood, rice, cooking oil, salt."

Raymond smiled.

"What?"

"Wedding parties for straight couples?" Now the bemused smile had gotten into Raymond's eyes.

Fong Mun laughed. "Yes."

They laughed not knowing what exactly was so funny.

Raymond turned to the screen. "You don't do any more gardening." He looked to Fong Mun. "Is there a reason?"

"The land. The soil had an unfamiliarity to it at first. Something I couldn't get hold of. The components. The dryness. The lettuce didn't grow. I tried other vegetables, like spinach and cabbage. They did poorly."

"You could have used plant food."

Fong Mun could say nothing to this. He stared at Raymond before going on. "I couldn't pry open the hardness of the land here." Fong Mun crossed his arms. "Climate is another factor. California summer dries everything; the hills turn brown, grass dies. I still don't know how the season works or how to till the Californian soil."

"You can buy soil in the stores." More suggestions. "A couple of dollars a bag."

A garden in pots? Fong Mun recoiled at the thought. "I don't know what month to sow seeds."

"You could have read gardening books."

Uhhhh . . . Fong Mun almost stuck fingers in his ears and screamed. Regardless of guides and instructions, I can't relate to the land here.

Noting Fong Mun's distress, Raymond leaned forward. "What kind of gardening did you do before?"

1975, Luang Prabang, Laos

In the photo shop, Fong Mun looked out the window across the courtyard. He stood watching his neighbor Uncle K. climb the coconut tree by his family's bathing stall. The tree was shorter than all the others that arched along the pond, far out to the sky.

"Young trees don't bear sweet coconuts. Why doesn't he listen?" Fong Mun turned to his grandmother.

At eighty, Ahma didn't need glasses. She wore her thick white hair almost shoulder-length, greased and combed backward, a clip above each ear. She sat in an armchair behind the display counter, her quick fingers counting cash receipts.

On the display counter—above the array of photos spread out under the glass tabletop—lay the Chinese newspaper, a few days old, with big headlines of the fighting in Vietnam and of mass live burials in Cambodia. So close to Laos. But Ahma couldn't read.

"We should leave him alone." She kept counting money.

"The tree's in our backyard!"

"How much can a few coconuts be worth? Leave him alone and tend to business."

"But I've planned to let them ripen." Fong Mun stamped his feet. "The tree's ours."

Ahma glanced past her fifteen-year-old grandson before turning to him. "Silly child, he just needs some money for cigarettes."

With a knife, a foot long, dark iron green, tied to his waist, Uncle K. shinnied his way up. He was tall and thin, long-limbed, long-faced, dark brown. He had a crew cut, half silver gray. His left arm circled the trunk while his right hand pulled out the knife and began to hack at the stem.

Fong Mun heard *thump thump thump*. Before long a stalk of four or five coconuts dropped with a heavy plop to the ground. Uncle K. shinnied down and towed the coconuts by the stalk past the bathing stall, across the Fongs' courtyard to his home.

"They'll taste sour," Fong Mun told Ahma, and cursed Uncle K. for taking away his coconuts. "The dead old head! Bad egg! Bad-luck ghost!"

In less than a week Fong Mun found Uncle K. on a tree again—the tall *mayom* tree. A walkway cut through the courtyard and connected the shop to the kitchen and the washing area. Half of the courtyard touched the sidewalk, and the other half—where the mayom tree grew—bordered on the K. family's hut.

Fong Mun, in the walkway, heard some swishing

17

and shaking of branches on the roof. He came to the yard. On the tree, Uncle K. was cutting the tender leaves with a sickle and letting them drop to the ground. The tree shed dry leaves all year long, and every morning the Fongs' maid swept them.

Uncle K. collected the young leaves and ignored tiny parts of twigs and the fruits on the ground.

Fong Mun did not claim the ownership of this tree. He saw it as his neighbor's because, first, its tiny fruits tasted sour and, second, he wanted the couple to do their share of sweeping. The hard yellow fruits dropped into the yard, but no one picked them up.

Because Fong Mun liked the orchid plant that grew on the tree trunk, he considered it as belonging to his family. The orchid faced the kitchen and the walkway, away from his neighbor's hut. He didn't know where the orchid came from or who had grafted it there. Uncle K. could not sell the stems of purple-black flowers for his cigarette money. No one had ever cut the flowers. So truly the orchid had no owner. It grew on the tree, received rain, and blossomed. In dry weather the orchid collected dust. Only then did it remind Fong Mun of the need to water the plant.

He connected the hose to the faucet at the bathing stall, towed the hose across the walkway to the yard. Under the tree, he squeezed the handle. A jet of water shot diagonally toward the tree trunk and the orchid, spraying its dusty leaves and its root nest. Dirty water dripped down. Fong Mun kept spraying until the water that dripped looked clear. Clusters of dark purple flowers dangled down in stems smooth like jade.

After Uncle K. had taken the *mayom* leaves to sell to the Vietnamese shopkeepers for use as wrapping for pickled meat roll, his wife stepped down from their hut with a broom in her hand.

Auntie K. was all wrinkles, her coarse skin clinging close to her bones. She swept only the leaves fallen on her side. Then, with the broom still in her hand, she crossed the courtyard. She laid the broom by the door and, lifting her sarong a few inches up her ankles, entered the kitchen.

Fong Mun noticed Auntie K.'s broom by the door as he headed for the kitchen. Just outside the door, he heard Ahma's voice: "Has not one-fourth of the pond been filled already? I know the landlord plans to build houses on that strip of new landfill."

He stepped in. Each of the two old women squatted on a low stool, surrounded by a stove with a few sticks of firewood, two cabinets, a chopblock, and, next to it, a row of bottles and glass containers—squid brand fish sauce, dark soy sauce, light soy sauce, vinegar, salted black beans. A layer of soot covered the ceiling and the walls.

"But you know why he stopped there?" Auntie K. leaned toward Ahma. "Because it disturbed the two serpents living in the pond—having rocks, debris, and earth dumped into their home. How will they put up with such pollution?"

Fong Mun never knew the pond had housed two serpents. He was about to ask Ahma if she knew, when Auntie K. pronounced, "Neighbors along the opposite side of the pond heard wails at midnight."

Fong Mun and Ahma exchanged glances: no such pond-side mourning had ever woken them. Twenty to thirty families lived along each of the two long sides of the rectangular pond. The shorter sides bordered on the streets. And the Fongs lived on a corner where the short and the long sides of the pond met.

"All night long, loud wails, nonstop," Auntie K. said. "The serpents have deserted the pond and have moved to the base of the Golden Pagoda Mountain, for a purer and more spiritual dwelling."

Fong Mun pictured two serpents as long as the tallest coconut trees rising out of the water from the center of the pond, rising above the roof of the three-story building known as the Lao-American Language Association, rising and twining, churning the water, making the duckweeds bob.

"Without our two spirit guardians, what will happen next?" Auntie K. asked.

Weeds spread over the new tract of land, where the landlord had filled one-fourth of the pond, along the street. Neighbors across the street dumped garbage there.

"It must stop," Fong Mun's father decreed. In his mid-forties, Mr. Fong had light skin—a result of working in the darkroom—and prominent black hair. "The land is not a garbage dump." He ordered his workers to buy bamboo to fence off the landfill.

The workers unloaded the bamboo from the truck and piled it in the courtyard. They spent the next few afternoons making the fence in the walkway outside the darkroom: sawing the bamboo to the desired length, splitting each segment in half, weaving the fence.

They erected the tall fence between the sidewalk and the field, what had been part of the pond, along the whole stretch of the sidewalk, all the way from the Fong residence to the border of a neighbor's home at the end of the block. When the weather turned cooler, this neighbor put up a fence perpendicular to the long row of fence Mr. Fong had built, and divided the field in half.

Fong Mun turned to Ahma. "Look at her." He pointed toward the field.

By the window behind the display counter, Ahma turned to look: the woman, the neighbor on the other side, was heaping weeds with a rake while her son chopped down more waist-tall weeds with a machete. She set fire to the mound of weeds.

In one path the smoke drifted across the field, over the fence, through the banana grove, and toward the window where Ahma and Fong Mun gathered. It comforted Ahma to know that someone finally did something with the junkyard.

Fong Mun ran to inform his mother. He swung the door open and entered the cool, dark bedroom next to Ahma's.

His mother had a perm, more gray than black. She wore a sleeveless flower-patterned blouse she had made herself. She had made her pants, too, soft and loose. She sat knitting an orange sweater for Fong Mun in an armchair, in front of her makeup table. To her right stood a shelf of back issues of *Family Living,* the magazine she subscribed to, which contained recipes. As she knit, the two long knitting needles in her stubby hands came together and then apart, each movement turning the spool of orange wool on her lap. A small patch—the beginning of a sweater—swayed between the two needles.

"Papa paid for the bamboo!" he yelled into her face.

"Just because your papa paid for it?" She frowned, leaning back to put more distance between herself and her son, setting the knitting needles down.

The sternness in her eyes puzzled Fong Mun. He opened his mouth, about to reason with her, when she leaned toward him. "You think the land belongs to you just because your papa paid for the fence?" She scowled at him. "So narrow-minded. So unkind." A slight tremor ran through her right hand, but she suppressed the rising impulse to slap him. "You never learn."

The snappishness of her tone made Fong Mun turn away and stomp toward the door. He yelled out as soon as the door swung shut behind him, "If she wants part of the land, why doesn't she pay for the fence too? Why did she wait until we put it up? I've never seen anything like this! Siding with outsiders!"

He dashed to Ahma by the window. Catching his breath, he turned back to look, but the door to his mother's chamber remained shut.

The neighbor worked in the field every afternoon. When it got too hot, at three, she went indoors for a rest and her son, wearing only shorts, would show up with a hoe balanced on his shoulder, to continue the work his mother had left off.

Standing by the window, Fong Mun watched the neighbor boy stooped over in the distant field. He had only seen him fully clothed, and the sight of the boy clad in shorts, sweating, drew Fong Mun to the window.

The neighbor boy worked a small area. He tilled and loosened the soil, sifted and cleared away glass shards and stones.

One day, in search of goose eggs in the field, Fong Mun was surprised to see, through the fence, young green shoots growing in a bed. The woman had built several other beds too. He also noticed that the neighbor boy's body had turned brown. Fong Mun took a deep breath.

On the other side of the fence, the neighbor did not see him, but Fong Mun quickly left the garden, as if the distance between them were too close. Fong Mun stopped under the short coconut tree behind the bathing stall, and watched from there.

Two weeks later, standing by the fence, Fong Mun saw the white roots of the parsnips, already plump, in the bed rich with moist and coal-black soil.

He set out to duplicate his neighbor's garden. First, the workers added another fence to block off three sides of the field—the fourth side bordered the pond. Then they built a door. With the geese warded off, Fong Mun started from the area with the moistest soil and the least weeds and debris.

He could never hoe deeply enough. Most of the time the hoe hit rocks, broken glass, and sticky brick-red clay. He couldn't seem to reach good soil. There were times when he wanted to have no more to do with the garden. But when he saw the parsnips of his neighbor growing ever stouter and whiter, he continued.

The roots of the weeds went deeper than his hoe could reach. So he pulled them with his hands, but found a reticular network, stout, hardy roots enmeshing each other over the land. He used a trowel to dig, cursing the strength of those roots. But if the weeds could grow so strong, the vegetables too could grow as strong. He worked for a week but completed only a small plot.

He found three workers sitting around by the bench in front of the darkroom, smoking and fanning themselves with their hats. He dragged a worker by the hand. "Come, come, I want you to pull the weeds."

"Maybe later," the worker said, withdrawing his hand. "Still too hot."

Fong Mun turned to pull another worker's hand. When none of them would move, he yelled, "Lazy— all of you! All you do is sit around!"

Mrs. Fong came to the door with a severe frown. "What are you yelling about?"

Fong Mun pouted. "They want to sit around not working."

"Work?" She raised her eyebrows. "You should do what you can and shouldn't order others to do work for you."

He stood with his feet apart, his head lifted and lips puckered.

"No one forces you to grow vegetables," she said.

He eyed her: true, no one forced him to work the junkyard, not Ahma and not his father.

"So if you want to have a garden, you'll have to work on it with your own hands," his mother said.

Without giving the lazy workers so much as a look, he turned his back and walked out.

He returned to the garden. He piled up broken Pepsi bottles, rocks, plastic bags with straws in them, weeds. He found a fat worm curled inside the damp, soft soil. "Lazy parasite, all you know is sleep," he grunted, and slit it with a stick, and it burst with a pop.

His parents showed up around four. They came near him. "What do you need done?"

Fong Mun pointed. "This area here."

His mother began to pull the weeds with her stubby hands. She couldn't shake loose the tough, stout weeds. So she used a trowel to turn up softer soil.

His father swung the hoe overhead and then dropped it with a thud, easy and quick. With each thud, the hoe reached deeply into the soil and turned up plastic bags, rusty cans, straws, stones, and fat weed roots.

Fong Mun stood by, ready to pick them apart, wondering if the neighbor boy would show up.

"Don't stand too near the hoe," Mr. Fong told his son. He hoed rapidly and covered a large area in twenty minutes. It would take Fong Mun the next two days to clean it up for the building of a bed.

Fong Mun grew garlic and shallots in the first bed, the easiest to grow. He picked cloves that already had shoots and stubby roots, stuck them in the soil, and watered them with the pond water. To expand his green venture, he sowed a variety of seeds: carrots, cabbages, tomatoes, cauliflowers, and spinach.

Some seeds sprouted after two days. New shoots stretched from the seeds; the roots stretched into the soil, the body stretched up. In the early morning Fong Mun went to check how much taller they had grown from the night before, certain that they were growing even as he watched them, lengthening downward and upward. A pair of leaves grew from each young shoot.

After a week a small forest of new growth covered the beds. Fong Mun patted them, his hands roving over the fluffy young plants, treating them like guests in his garden. When they got stronger, he would re-move each of them to a different bed, space them out in the eight long beds.

His hand had reached the garden door when Fong Mun spotted, in the distance, Auntie K. tilling the field with a hoe. She had taken the farthest end where the neighbor who grew parsnips had fenced off the land.

How could she simply show up, without permis-sion from his family, without dropping so much as a word? She had even erected a small fence. Surely to mark the property line?

Rushing indoors, he ran head-on into his mother.

After listening to his account, Mrs. Fong raised her eyebrows. "You can't even take care of your own little piece, whining about work, and now you want to take up the whole plot."

He stamped his feet. "No one can touch mine!"

"Yours? What is yours? You tell me." She eyed him sternly.

"The whole thing!"

"You want to take everything. Can you handle the whole piece by yourself? Can you?"

Ahma came in. "She doesn't have enough to feed her family. Look at her children. The two boys don't even have shoes. So let her use the land."

"You mean she can just show up and take half the garden?"

"Still talking back? You?" Mrs. Fong turned around, her hand raised, and Fong Mun hushed.

He bolted into the bedroom, slammed the door, but no sooner did the door swing shut than his mother charged after him.

Her right hand raised, she chased him. He ran, flew out of his slippers, and jumped onto the bed. She yelled, "You're dirtying the bed, you!" He ran over the sheets to the other side. She lurched toward him and he jumped again, reaching for the door.

He rushed to the hallway and she leaped after him. But she stopped chasing him. He turned around: she had stopped in the doorway with one foot on the threshold, her eyes glazed, her gaze fixed on a leather-case radio on the photographer's worktable.

The radio emitted a loud scratchy sound. The photographer employee, Uncle Woo, ears pricked up, eyeballs bulged, sat by the window listening intently to the radio in front of him, the antenna already pulled all the way up.

The report from Saigon sounded clear one moment and blurred and jumbled the next.

Fong Mun looked away from Uncle Woo toward the front door. Across the hall, Ahma stood by the front door, her eyes, too, fixed on the radio. Her rush to intercept the chase between her daughter-in-law and her grandson—in other words, to spoil him once again by saving him from punishment—came to a halt.

Fong Mun turned around, only to find his father, whose face was tense with rage, heading toward him. But halfway to his son, the father, too, stopped, his ears pricked up, his eyes turned to the radio, his rush to discipline his son suspended.

All stood still listening to the jarring, jumbled Mandarin of the newsman reporting live from Saigon. The city had fallen.

Did Raymond detect a "delicate" feel to the Web site, too, the "soft voice" of the cook?

Raymond continued to browse the site. It showed a California garden with sunshine and the open space that housed the variety of roses destined for the bouquets and table centerpieces of straight newlyweds.

"The gardeners take care of the orchids and roses," said Fong Mun. "The plumeria didn't do well. Again it's the soil, the climate."

Raymond mentioned the plumeria tree in the Berkeley Botanical Garden.

"In the tropical greenhouse?"

Raymond nodded. "I like to go there."

This piece of news brought relief to Fong Mun. This young man, whose notion of gardening consisted of plant food and soil that came in bags, still had a need to experience something of Southeast Asia, to relive a sense of that land.

Raymond admitted to knowing little about Laos. The virtual world of Laos he built began with a fist (like the shape of the country) which morphed into the poor country found on the map.

"You left there at a very young age. Weren't you four at the time?"

"Yes—but tell me, why did you switch from gardening to catering?"

Fong Mun made note of Raymond's rush to change the subject. Sensitive about the disappearance of his father, perhaps? To put Raymond at ease, Fong Mun ignored the abrupt shift and talked on. "Out of necessity. I once tried to grow vegetables outdoors. Ants carried away the seeds. And when the remainders sprouted, bugs ate them. This is a harsh environment, let me tell you."

Fong Mun expected a response such as "Why didn't you use some bug killers?" but Raymond remained silent. An awkward pause followed, and it alarmed Fong Mun. At the dinner party he had felt connected to Raymond, bound by a sense of shared community. Unlike others, this community so far had only two members: he and Raymond.

Other gay communities, such as the Vietnamese, were large enough to form alliances (in California at least), hold meetings and events, and make mailing lists available on the Internet. The straight Chinese had their own groups, too, based on regions. Fong Mun recognized the dialects they spoke. He too spoke Cantonese and Mandarin, but he came from neither Hong Kong, Taiwan, or Mainland China. Neither would he fit in a Laotian group, whose vision and rituals were geared strictly toward straights. Plus, his knowledge of Chinese would make him less Laotian in the eyes of some. It partly explained why he preferred to deal with people on a business basis, concerned only with debit and credit.

Fong Mun realized he must now make an effort. Must continue to speak and engage Raymond's attention. Must keep this new member in his half-formed community. Fong Mun broke the silence. "I didn't know what to do, in spite of reading gardening books. I had no garden. Those early years in California, living in apartments and moving from place to place, made me feel disconnected from the land. At one point I used milk cartons to grow some lettuce indoors. Even then the aphids infested the area." He took a deep breath. "I had not even unpacked before we had to leave again. Over time I developed this mind-set—always ready to move. Didn't bother to unpack. The environment—the apartments, the backyards—became temporary. I had no sense of home, no feelings for the land. People and places, they come and go. All sojourners. Cooking became the only constant, my one connection to—"

"So it leads you to the hospitality business."

At once, Fong Mun's sense of alarm vanished. At least Raymond is still awake, he thought, and sighed with relief. "I'm just a caterer." He now realized that this young man could talk and think as much about "firewood, rice, cooking oil, salt" as he did, and a sense of sympathy filled Fong Mun's eyes.

"It's why you give dinner parties," Raymond said.

Fong Mun nodded. Entertaining people with food had provided him with a way to become a host and thus to nurture himself.

Raymond smiled. "Nothing beats the egg rolls you make."

"It connects me to a familiar world. I can even catch the aroma when I crave the seafood egg rolls my grandmother made. I began to duplicate the steps in my head. I saw her hands mixing the ingredients. She must have set out to make egg rolls for the same reason as me, caught in nostalgia."

Raymond looked intent.

Fong Mun drew a deep breath. Keep talking. "As she mixed the ingredients, she thought about her younger days. When I make seafood egg rolls, I remember how she went over each step, the way she learned it in Hanoi, before she fled to Laos in the fifties. But in 1975, the government stopped the import of seafood . . ." And then Fong Mun saw, in the distance, a huge red wave swooping down toward him with all of its powerful, engulfing force.

1975, Luang Prabang, Laos

It tumbled from the hillside where the *lycée* and the *collège* stood. It flung open the gates of these schools and swept down the hill, to the town, picking up force as it came.

Nine o'clock. The day had barely started: some townspeople had just gotten up.

The red crest rode downhill and caught the first block of town, the section that stood in its patch, by surprise. Before the wide-eyed, mouth-agape residents of the first block could even blink, the wave turned the corner and reached for the next.

It rode toward an ancient temple called Wat Visoon. Some apprentice monks there were carrying pails of water from the well by the bodhi tree to the kitchen, and some were getting their equipment ready to build a tomb, mixing cement with sand and water, while inside the monastery rows of advanced monks sat meditating in the lotus position.

Jolted from their meditation on impermanence, the advanced monks opened their eyes. The apprentice monks suspended their activities as well. As they all wondered—what was that roar, that upturn?—the red wave flooded past the temple toward the Sound of the Celestial, one of the two cinema houses in town.

It filled the empty, musty cinema house with such clamor that the janitor, who had just gone in to sweep the floor, thought that a movie was playing, a battle scene. But he looked up to find a blank screen. He turned around but saw no one in the projection booth. He thought of those who, a year ago, had died in the theater during the two grenade explosions, caused by drunken soldiers in a brawl. Suddenly the janitor had a vision of the dead watching the movie when the grenade blew them limbless, their blood splattered on the walls.

The sound came louder than ever, so loud that the janitor, a Buddhist who never doubted that he could always answer for his conscience, finally came to his senses and made out that the sound came from outside, from the street, and not from the haunted projection booth, where the dead were cranking the projector, replaying the film. By the time the janitor opened a side door to peek out, he saw only the rear of the wave, for the frontal crest had reached the Lao-American Language Association, half a block up from the Sound of the Celestial.

Inside the three-story building of the Language Association, the Americans thought the uproar resulted from the solar eclipse, the town banging pots and pans as darkness came over the sun. But instead of hearing the banging of utensils, the Americans heard kicks on the door, objects thrown against it, shouts that came to their ears like curses; and they saw figures through door slits, and they averted their eyes. This time they all knew that the sense of unrest that had long plagued their minds had materialized.

The red wave took a turn around the corner, and that was when Ahma, in the kitchen, first heard its crashing. She had just returned from the market and sat down to chop a slice of pork.

Doubting her ears, she stood up from the low stool, wondering whether that could be it: it had come to her mind lately and she knew it was only a matter of time before the Communists followed at her heels and again brought disaster to her as they had twenty years ago. She knew what Mr. Woo, the photographer, listened to on the radio: the daily reports from Vietnam and Cambodia. On the way to the kitchen, she had passed by Mr. Woo's worktable: she had seen the newspaper on his table and, on the front page, pictures of carnage in Cambodia. Truckloads of people being sent off. Men and women lining up outside a trench before they were forced into it and buried alive. A heap of bodies lying on the roadside. Ahma knew Laos would be next.

She got out of the kitchen and came muttering to the front of the shop. The wave of student demonstrators surged toward her. "We demand freedom!" "We want emancipation!" Their shouts rose over her, drowning her sense of hearing. She retreated to her room. "Stay there, don't go anywhere," her son yelled from the door. She didn't hear him as she clutched her long, round prayer string. Luckily her grandson was in school.

The protesters poured into the shop. With angry eyes, they swung their clenched fists in the air, spat out hateful words. They knocked down the waste basket and spilled its contents. They pounded on the walls, jumped on the counter, stamped their feet. A young man shook the glass showcase until all the photos and frames fell. A woman pounded on the sign and cried, "Down with capitalism!"

The red wave surged over the street and pulled down the fence that Mr. Fong had built. Two or three planks came loose from the fence and were swept adrift. A few rocks were thrown into the courtyard, startling the chickens. The chickens flocked to the back, under Auntie K.'s hut. The wave rode on, to a nearby royal officer's house, to the market.

As they cleared away the waste papers, beer cans, and other debris littering the shop and re-erected the photos and frames in the showcase, the workers grumbled: "The Russians planned this." "They egg on the students."

In Fong Mun's garden, the cabbages curled into tight balls; the cauliflowers, at first a nebula of white, grew into umbrellas of yellow; the toothpick roots of carrots turned orange and grew long and thicker. Unravaged by the wave that emancipated the kingdom, the vegetables had drawn nutrients from it and flourished.

One morning on his way to the garden, Fong Mun saw a figure through the fence. He opened the door, stepped in, and found Auntie K. building two more beds in the middle of his garden.

Fong Mun ran to the kitchen to inform Ahma. Seated by the chopblock, she eyed him for an unnerving interval.

"The land doesn't belong to us." She went on to tell him that the K.'s were the distant relatives of the landlord. "So they can do pretty much what they want with the property, such as taking the coconuts to sell. The auntie who grows parsnips is a relative of the landlord too, a close one. We don't own the land. We don't own the house we live in. Neighbors have as much right to the land as we do."

Fong Mun gaped. Whenever Ahma mentioned the landlord, he thought she referred to the neighbors', for he always had regarded his father as the host of the house, a landlord rather than a tenant. Now he realized his family were "paying guests" like Mr. Woo. Mr. Woo had no family and thus had to rely on the goodwill of his employer for room and board. Mr. Woo's quest for a better life had taken him from his native China to South Vietnam as a young man, and then on to Laos. He had found employment, but had ended up a homeless, country-less middle-aged bachelor. Now in the walkway Fong Mun glanced at the fenced-in garden behind the bathing stall, the fruit trees in the courtyard, the tile-roof house that was the photo shop: his home belonged to a faceless entity called the landlord. He stepped back. From then on the distance between his house and him began to widen.

Auntie K. showed some zest at first for tending her part of the garden, growing lettuce, shallots, cilantro, and chilies on the beds that she had mustered her strength to plow. Sometimes for days she did not come to water. Maybe she forgot, or was lazy or tired. She showed up to water less often. Then she stopped going to the garden altogether. The lettuces wilted before they turned wood brown, and then flowered, but bore no seeds. Weeds took over.

At the end, Fong Mun had the garden to himself. But his mother was right: it was too large for him to tend.

"I'm not done yet. Can't you see?"

"Come in," Ahma called, standing with arms akimbo by the banana grove. "The sky has turned dark. Dinner will get cold."

"I still have a lot to do," Fong Mun shouted over the fence.

He went on watering the vegetables.

"Come in."

Fong Mun ignored Ahma and carried the empty can to the pond to refill it.

"Your father is getting the stick," Ahma called again.

Fong Mun laid down the watering can and left the garden. On the way to the dining table, he grunted, "No one helps me. I have to do everything by myself." His stomach growled. When he saw that dinner had started without him, he grouched, "I wouldn't have to work so late if someone helped me."

He sat down next to Ahma, took up the bowl of rice that Ahma had filled for him. As he chewed the first mouthful, he felt a sting on his leg. He slapped the itchy spot and became even more irritated when the mosquito flew away, free to sting him again.

Auntie K.'s eighteen-year-old daughter, Junda, appeared in the courtyard. She hurried past the kitchen holding in her arms a basket of water spinach. Her two younger brothers, a few years old, barefoot, trotted closely behind her.

Fong Mun slammed his bowl and chopsticks on the table and cried out, "How can she walk in and take the water spinach? How dare she?"

"We don't want it anyway," Ahma said. "It grows wild in the pond. So let her."

"I won't have it! I'll kick her away the next time I see her coming in. I'll block the door—"

"How can you talk like this?" Fong Mun's mother glared at him, her chopsticks held in midair. And his father fetched the bamboo stick from a beam below the eaves in the dining area.

Fong Mun ignored the stick and went on airing his temper.

"Get out to the yard," his father ordered.

Fong Mun stayed still.

"Move!"

The holler startled Fong Mun. His father stood up.

Fong Mun, without a word, quickly got up and made for the yard. His father bolted madly after him.

He had barely reached the yard, under the canopy of the *mayom* tree, when he saw several quick flashes of white cutting across his eyes right and left. He flinched, writhed. Tears flooded over his eyes before he felt the pain eating into his legs.

Just as quickly, Mr. Fong put the stick back in its place, returned to the table, sat down, continued his dinner.

"Stop crying now," Ahma called. "Come back to the table and eat."

"Stand there," Mr. Fong ordered. "No dinner for him."

Fong Mun cried freely under the tall old tree.

"Your eyes will bulge like a melon if you keep on," Ahma said.

Everyone else at the table continued dinner.

The next morning, when Fong Mun was in school, the Brothers—the Lao Cong, the Comrades—marched into the Fongs' home to count trees. When they marched in, Ahma was in the kitchen chopping meat and Mrs. Fong sat in an armchair by the entrance to the photo studio knitting the orange sweater.

As she knit, Mrs. Fong heard boots crunching on the sidewalk. She had barely glanced up when the Brothers stepped in.

Hands crossed behind them like a pair of open scissors, they stopped by the front counter, but not to look at the photographs on display. A Brother cleared his throat, stepped past the counter toward Mrs. Fong, and told her in a flat, firm voice what they came for.

In the kitchen, Ahma had laid down her knife by the chopblock. She had seen through the door the three Brothers on the sidewalk heading toward the shop—of course they could be going to the market and needed to pass the shop. But their presence brought a sense of foreboding to her. Ever since the morning of the student protest her temples had throbbed like an alarm going off—even in her sleep.

Just as Ahma rose to her feet, the three Brothers crossed the threshold, one after the other, into the walkway that cut through the courtyard and led to the kitchen. Behind the Brothers followed Mrs. Fong. Ahma stepped over the kitchen door into the walkway. "What is it?" she asked.

"We have an assignment." The unsmiling Brother rattled off. "As a part of the project to assess our beloved country's natural resources, we are ordered to record the number and the specimen of trees and livestock in this household." He opened a binder.

Ahma noticed that they had seen the chicken coop and the chickens and geese in the yard.

The Brothers, proceeding from the right side of the courtyard, observed the mango tree bearing tiny mangoes. The Brothers turned their eyes to another young mango tree, which had germinated three years ago when Fong Mun, upon finishing a mango, had thrown the seed in the courtyard.

A Brother jotted something down. The visitors ducked under the clotheslines stretching over the yard, passed the large tank of water in the bathing stall, and came to the banana grove. One Brother, unaware of

41

Ahma's glare, counted the banana trees with his fingers.

Wherever they went, Ahma followed closely, while Mrs. Fong watched from the walkway.

In front of Mrs. Fong was a small fenced-in area where she had tried growing potatoes, which never produced any leaves, and durian, two seeds of which had germinated and grown to the height of a new pencil, but no higher. The durian had not survived the cool weather—just as well, else the Brothers would have noticed and questioned the Fongs for their extravagance: eating durians, the imported king of fruits, at a time when the stomachs of the peasants growled.

The Brothers passed the banana grove and came near the coconut tree that Uncle K. had climbed. The vegetable garden came into view: the bedful of garlic, lettuce, tomato, and pepper plants behind the fence. The Brothers sidestepped the coconut tree and went to the fence to open the garden door.

When the Brothers returned from the garden, one told Mrs. Fong about the night seminars. "Every housewife in the district has to go." They stood in the walkway, near the darkroom.

Mrs. Fong turned pale. Ahma cast a glance at her and could not bear the thought of her getting brainwashed, the teachings of Marx, Lenin, and Mao being expounded to her. Ahma took a step forward, to get in between the Brothers and Mrs. Fong. But what if the Brothers put her on the list for the seminar too—for the brainwash? Ahma stood still.

After the Brothers left, Ahma returned to the

kitchen trembling, and by the chopblock she sighed. "They'll starve us all."

Ahma went to different butchers, who by then either had run out of stock or were allotted only a certain amount to sell per week. Prices jumped. As soon as she got word, she filled her pockets with cash and went to the butchers. She paid five thousand kips for five kilos of beef. She cut it up in small chunks so that they fit in the cylindrical ice chest among ice chunks.

Meat dishes turned up on the dining table: stir-fried beef for lunch, steamed ground pork with tofu for dinner, steamed spareribs in salted black bean for next day's lunch, stewed beef for dinner. For variety? Fish and chicken.

Sure, Mr. Fong needed his daily intake of meat to build muscle, and Fong Mun needed to eat meat to grow. And Mrs. Fong, and Ahma, and even the employee Mr. Woo, the photographer for whom the Fongs provided room and board: everyone needed to eat meat. No one could argue with that. But they could only eat so much. Sometimes a dish looked untouched when Ahma brought it back to the kitchen.

Ahma kept turning out meat dishes. Parcels of meat crowded inside the ice chest and pushed over the lid. She took out the ice to make room for the meat she'd ordered.

For two weeks the butcher stands remained closed. It confirmed her worst fear: what she had spent her life running from, the days of organized famine, had arrived.

At the end of the third week, as soon as she got word that a water buffalo would be killed, she hurried to the butcher.

The Brothers, too, got word. They sauntered into the slaughterhouse but found it empty and neat, no live water buffalo or traces of recent killing, no dark purple spots on the ground, beside the trough, or along the pen. They sniffed but caught no stink of blood. They searched the sty but found neither pigs nor water buffaloes.

The Brothers threw a look at the butcher, who stood with his hands crossed behind his back, his head bowed, smiling most obligingly.

Ahma hurried into the slaughterhouse.

The Brothers turned and saw what they took to be an old Vietnamese woman standing in the doorway. It was Ahma's typically Vietnamese outfit—white blouse worn over a pair of shiny, wide-legged black pants— the outfit Ahma wore 365 days a year, that gave that impression. The Brother in the middle smiled to himself and turned to face the butcher.

The butcher opened his mouth to speak, but the Brother got ahead of him. "We've been here long enough, brother," he said, patting the butcher on the shoulder. "We don't want to keep you from your work." The Brother stressed the last word as he stood in front of the butcher, eye to eye.

The butcher turned pale.

As the Brothers filed out, slinging their rifles on their shoulders, they didn't nod to Ahma. At the door the Brother who had patted the butcher on the shoulder turned around and fixed him with a stare. "We hope to see you on the next visit," he said.

After the Brothers had gone, the butcher turned to face Ahma. "It'll have to wait awhile."

She sighed and sat down on a chair. She placed her right elbow on the armrest and began to rub her hands while gazing at the earthen floor.

"It's not so bad," the butcher said. "They just want to keep the water buffalo for the rice field. These cavemen don't know what they are doing."

The butcher had known Ahma for over twenty years. Refugees, they had fled from Vietnam to Laos in the mid-1950s. They drove from the capital of Laos to Luang Prabang. A procession of cars, trucks, and buses crossed the highlands. The young Mr. Fong drove the Green Fishtail, the stalwart Ahma seated beside him. In a rackety bus, a young man who in later years took up the butcher's trade peeked out a window. A flock of birds and butterflies of every description flapped their wings and flew alongside the human train that wound its way around the narrow mountain road, up and down the hills.

"Whatever happened to the Green Fishtail?" the Butcher asked, seeking refuge from the tense present in the wonders of long ago.

"The rusty old car? It sits in the garage collecting spider webs." Gazing at the earthen floor, Ahma rubbed her chapped hands.

"Easy now. Wait a few days," the butcher whispered.

Two days later, in an afternoon chat at the market,

a Vietnamese *pho* vendor leaned close to Ahma and whispered, "The butcher killed another water buffalo last night. My daughter heard the howl."

Ahma put her fan down, stood upright from the bench, took leave, and headed for the butcher.

He sold her two kilos.

She put the meat in the ice chest but found room for more meat. She fingered the long, round string of prayer beads, round after round.

It took another month before a parcel of fresh meat came into her hands.

As she fingered the prayer beads behind the counter, praying to keep the Brothers away, they stepped into the shop, bringing the smell of caves with them. During the war, the American bombing had sent the Brothers into hiding in the caves up north. Now, after the emancipation, or the so-called Bloodless Revolution, they came to town. And their newly won liberation led them, in groups of twenty or thirty, to the front of the photo shop. And with a sense of childlike wonder they admired the displayed photos.

All of them set their mind on having their pictures taken. Seated behind the counter, Ahma looked sullen. She wouldn't look at them. When they asked her about the prices of the different sizes of photos, she pretended she didn't hear them. Instead she said the photographer was taking an afternoon nap. They didn't seem to understand her, which was the equivalent of ignoring her: captured by the power of photography, they were heedless of her treatment of them. They were ready to spend money.

They gathered in front of the counter while a few strayed to the studio, gravitating toward the camera set on the tripod. But no sooner did two Brothers peek into the camera than Ahma, undaunted, charged through the crowd to guard the prized equipment. The rest of the group followed her jauntily into the studio and in so doing—and to Ahma's dismay—discovered the dressing room. Now nothing short of a complete group photo could make them go away.

In the dressing room, their guffaws and the mildewed smell of caves woke up the photographer. His watch read one o'clock. He opened his bedroom door and entered the studio.

Ahma scowled at the Brothers: See what you've done; you've disturbed the requisite nap of the artist.

On his way to take a quick shower before starting work, the photographer told the Brothers to spruce themselves up for the photo session. They gladly obliged him.

Ahma slumped in a chair. The fact that they had breached her defense and succeeded in invading the dressing room further convinced her of the protean omnipresence of her foe, her nemesis.

In the dressing room, the Brothers spent a long time in front of the mirror turning their faces this way and that and dabbing their hair with water from a large tin cup by the mirror. They freely made use of the set of combs by the cup. The tin cup ran out of water:

dandruff and hair oil thickly lined the teeth of the combs.

The outcome: Ahma's appointed "artist," Mr. Woo, used up two rolls of film. A group photo was among the favorite. Arms on each other's shoulders, the Brothers allowed Mr. Woo to adjust their pose, guide them to look into the camera with a smile; Mr. Woo then brought the accordion lens into focus, turned on one or two strobe lights, and clicked the shutter. After Mr. Woo clicked the shutter, they still stood there smiling, basking in the spotlight, until Mr. Woo turned off the light. One Brother had Mr. Woo take five pictures of him, in different poses, of course. A soldier's pose. A side view of him gazing dreamily ahead, to convey the prospect of a college graduate. A full-body view of him standing with lifted chest and arms crossed, to portray a bodybuilder. A view of him sitting with a hand touching his chin: the image of a Laotian romantic. A closeup to announce the availability of a bachelor.

For the first time in their lives, the Brothers had a taste of happiness that came from the satisfaction of spending money. But surely they spent it, as the Fongs received it, with the implicit understanding that it would become a worthless wad in the near future? And surely Mr. Fong converted the currency to U.S. dollars and gold.

It was a period of unprecedented growth for the photo shop, as more Brothers arrived in town eager to be immortalized on film.

The position of Mr. Woo in the family began to

rise, because he became the only person to take pictures, while Mr. Fong worked exclusively in the darkroom, preferring to develop film and photographs in darkness rather than interacting with the Brothers in broad daylight. But Mr. Woo's unofficial status as an artist—the master of the old-fashioned box camera—was the result of Ahma's gold lust, for she confused the craftsmanship of a competent employee (her "cash cow," Mr. Woo) with the artistry of an auteur. It did not occur to her that the effects her son, Mr. Fong, produced in the darkroom made him an artist. To a mother, a son always remained a son, her "cash cow" by birthright rather than an artist by choice.

"Your grandmother is narrow-minded, mean to customers," Fong Mun's mother had told him. "She notices only the mess the customers make. If the combs remain clean, they're unused. Which means we don't have customers. She should see the dirty combs as a sign of booming business."

On another occasion, while a group of cave Brothers "spruced themselves up" (as the "artist" had put it), Ahma was chopping meat by the kitchen door. Perhaps the water in the tin cup had run low; perhaps the weather was too sweltering. In any case, one of the Brothers found his way to the tank of drinking water in the bathing stall.

The caveman picked up a pail and scooped it in the clear stream. Dousing his face, he splashed water all over the area.

Ahma poked her head out the door. She glared at

him, begrudging his trespass and the use of her water, but she caught the glint of the pistol around his belt.

Even so, her temper got the better of her, and she would have gone over to the Communist Brother, the likes of whom she had spent her life running away from, and she would have corrected his manners, had her son not come to the customer's rescue in time.

Mr. Fong stepped into the kitchen. "Leave him alone," he told Ahma in Cantonese, a tongue he knew the caveman by the tank would not grasp. "Don't the chores keep you busy enough? Just mind your business."

Mr. Fong had repeatedly told Ahma to treat customers like guests, to be broad-minded like the devout Buddhist she was, not to concern herself with the Brothers, whatever they did in preparing themselves for the camera. Let them splash water on their faces as much as they liked—the water would refresh them for the photo session. So look past them. Pretend ignorance. Fix her eyes on the chopblock and her energy on the chopping. Be blind to them. Or else go to the convent, talk to the nuns. Anything but lose sleep over the whims of the guests who, upon emancipation, had flooded down in waves from the caves up north.

Ahma darted a look at her son.

"Why waste your breath? Save it when you still can." He threw a glance at the caveman, who was still splashing away. Mr. Fong kept telling Ahma to save her breath, to conserve her *chi*. He didn't mean to curse, he dared not, but sometimes his temper, his exasperation, got the better of him. Before stepping out, he said, "You'll get in trouble with the authorities."

A few months before, he had spent a morning developing photos in the darkroom. As he opened the door to step out, he saw the Brothers counting trees in the courtyard, Ahma glaring at them, and his wife watching in the walkway. Normally, as the man of the house, he would have come forward to handle the matter, but an impulse—a combination of caution, prudence, and fear?—had hooked onto this ankles, his heels, and stopped him. He shut the door and stayed in the darkroom.

A few minutes later he reopened the door to peek out but was startled by the voices of the Brothers so nearby. They had not seen him behind the door listening to them tell his wife that she had to attend a night seminar.

Because glaring at her son or even at the cavemen failed to appease her, Ahma gritted her teeth. Only after her son and the Brothers had gone away did she begin to let loose what had built up in her bosom: by herself in the kitchen, she mumbled angry words while chopping the meat with quick loud thuds, words that by degrees got louder than the blows she dealt upon the meat. And in the evening another meat dish would appear on the table.

After dinner Ahma pulled out the drawer behind the counter and dug out an armful of cash filled with the smell of the cave. She carried the cash to her room and laid it in her bed. Inside the mosquito net, she sat cross-legged, counted the kips, sorted them into piles of one hundred, two hundred, five hundred, and a thousand, and tied each pile with a rubber band.

"Business. What business?" She said to Auntie K. afterward in the kitchen. "All the kips will become waste paper once they change the currency." Then she spoke loudly, as loudly as her conscience would allow her, so neighbors across the street, or passersby on the sidewalk, or customers in the shop, especially the Brothers eager to pose for the camera, could hear her declaration. "We have no business at all. Bad times. The cash drawer is empty. We're starving now. We drink a lot of water like everybody else."

For the Brothers she put on a weary look, the yoke of her life weighing more than the laborers', the peasants', and the water buffaloes'. When the Brothers came in to pick up their photos, they would see a hoary-headed, furrowed, dried-up "Vietnamese" grandma in a blouse yellowed with age and flappy, shiny black pants huddled by a drawer behind the counter, an octagenarian fingering the string of prayer beads for a futile purpose.

"The government changed the school system after the emancipation," Fong Mun told Raymond. "I got transferred to a new school and found myself in the same class as the neighbor boy in the garden."

"The same class!" Raymond exclaimed.

The neighbor boy became the class leader. After the reform, students spent more time on communal activities than in the classroom. The principal had converted the land behind the school into a communal garden. Working there in the afternoon, instead of attending classes, was mandatory.

In the sun the older students carried buckets to water the hard brown soil. Fong Mun stooped down with the girls around a bed they had worked on, each person holding a trowel. As he dug into the hard soil, he turned. At a near distance, Boontong—the head of the class, the neighbor boy—was pumping water.

"His shirt and dark green military pants are partially wet," Fong Mun told Raymond. "Water drips from his hair. I wait to see if he would do something about his shirt. It clings to his body, outlines his shape. His brown forearms glimmer with wetness."

Did the girls notice? Fong Mun glanced at them. They chatted and dug the trowels into the soil, mouths and hands all busy.

"None of them paid attention to him," Fong Mun said. "If only they knew what went on inside me! I liked to look at him, and yet I avoided getting too close to him. Too close to his body. The second half of his name, 'Tong,' means 'copper'—just like his skin, the blessed coppertone. At that time the principal turned every activity into a communal one, and attendance was mandatory—including even the botany teacher's wedding. So I saw him a lot. The Blessed Copper. But I avoided him. We hardly spoke to each other."

At the wedding, the students were not guests but workers behind the scene. On that morning, at the teacher's home, the class gathered in the kitchen and without instruction knew what to do. The girls washed vegetables, boiled water. The boys axed the firewood, built a fire, split the coconuts to halves with a thick knife, scraped them to hairlike fineness. Boontong straddled the scraper and began to shred the coconuts with quick, powerful strokes.

"From the wedding I got the recipe for my favorite coconut-chili-peanut fish soup."

Raymond said, "It sure sounds yummy."

"A Laotian dish," Fong Mun said. "My favorite.

At first I didn't know what my classmates were doing; so I just sat on a stool watching them work. My eyes often followed the movement of Boontong."

A girl soaked a bagful of dry chilies in warm water. Another added hot water to the shredded coconut and squeezed the mixture to extract the cream. The water became milky. She filtered the coconut cream, saved it in a bowl. She repeated the procedure, and the liquid, now more diluted, became the soup base. A girl added lime leaves, stalks of lemon grass, and slices of galinga—a kind of ginger—to the soup. One girl chopped the soaked chilies until they became fine and pasty. Another roasted peanuts in a wok. After they turned brown, she let them cool. Afterwards she rubbed them, to peel the skins: then she ground them with a pestle in a mortar. A girl boiled a few catfish, deboned them, ground them in a mortar with a pestle until mushy. Another girl heated up the thick coconut cream in a wok, brought it to a boil, added the chili paste.

Soon the chili cream emitted a spicy tang, and a thick layer of rich red oil gathered at the frothy surface. Everyone began to sneeze. A girl covered her nose and, with fortitude, transferred the spicy coconut chili cream to the boiling soup. She sneezed again, one last time. She added the ground peanuts and the fish to the soup. It produced an inviting aroma that displaced the spicy tang in the air. As the soup boiled, the aroma of coconut cream, peanuts, lime leaves, and galinga became stronger, the hallmark of the coconut-chili-peanut fish soup—served with rice noodles and raw vegetables like mint and thinly shredded cabbage.

"I then realized the class all along had been making my favorite food, reserved for the wedding guests yet to arrive."

Raymond asked, "Did you put it in the cookbook?"

Fong Mun nodded.

"We should make it sometime," Raymond said.

Fong Mun nodded again. He had high regard for someone whose words solidified what they promised or claimed, instead of turning into worthless prattle, into air. Words had the weight of gold, and for someone who followed up his words with action, it showed character. How much easier they were talking now, Fong Mun reflected. Words came easily. Whether they solidified into gold remained to be tested.

1975, Luang Prabang, Laos

The botany teacher was halfway through drawing a peanut plant on the chalkboard when the class heard footfalls—a pair of boots marching toward the classroom.

A tall, older student in military boots appeared at the door. Without giving the class so much as a glance, he strode up to the teacher and whispered to her. Her hand stopped on the board, in the midst of drawing peanuts attached to a cluster of roots. The student turned around and hurried off as abruptly as he had shown up, again without regarding those around him.

The teacher threw the chalk on her desk. Her face blank, she told the class to get ready.

The interruption had become routine. Other students were leaving their classrooms and crowding the long hallway.

Fong Mun in the back row put his notebook under the desk.

"Hurry up!" Boontong jumped to his feet and yelled. "Hurry."

The teacher hurried and stood by the door. She and the class followed Boontong—who charged with bold strides in his military boots, his head lifted high—to the school ground.

Fong Mun had gotten used to Boontong's sternness—the way he thundered at his fellow classmates and even the teacher, commanding them. Not the brightest, Boontong was the tallest, had the loudest voice and the coldest eyes. He also had flexibility: first he renounced his former education, which had trained him to salute the portrait of the king; then he took up communism, that fresh emancipator which demanded he remove the stale portrait of the king, if not the king himself. Boontong and others like him allied themselves with the new school principal, who appreciated young people of vision and gave them great authority as the heads of their respective classes.

The students lined up in front of the flagpole and the podium. The heads of all the classes, with hands crossed behind their straight backs, eyes alert for any signs of misbehavior from their nonvisionary classmates and teachers, marched back and forth in their military boots, at the front and the back of the assembly.

Ten minutes passed . . . twenty minutes. The botany teacher began to sweat and used a kerchief to fan her neck—a simple act which Boontong would write up as a sign of impatience and indulgence in the old way of life. After half an hour of standing in the sun,

Fong Mun felt the need to crouch down for a rest in the shade. Boontong would have interpreted the act as a lack of stamina and attention, lack of commitment to the Party. How could others stand for so long without signs of fatigue, but with increasing endurance?

Students in the back began to whisper. The whispering grew louder. Boontong turned around and swept his classmates with a sharp glance. The whispering stopped. He began to patrol the back.

After some lapse of time—the next period would have begun already—a figure cut across the front row and stepped up to the podium, behind the lectern. It was the school principal.

Himself a Brother, with a dark bronze face, the principal claimed to be self-educated, to have wallowed in the study of political doctrines while enduring years of hardship in the caves, and trying to dodge the B-52 carpet bombing from the United States. He sneered at his predecessor: a scholar pale and out of shape, his body weakened by years spent in the indulgence of book learning, his mind drugged by years of communion with Marcel Proust and the heroes of the Hindu epics. The principal stood behind the lectern, opened a booklet, and began pounding the new virtue into the students and the unenlightened teachers from the old system. Speaking with the kind of accent a bumpkin had, he cited from Marx and Lenin, and often referred to the two as one entity: Marx Lenin, "Marx" pronounced as "Mark," which sounded like the Lao word for "fruit." The fruit named Lenin. The Lenin fruit.

The lecture turned into an all-morning event in

the school grounds, where all stood hushed under the sun. The principal kept on propagating the virtues of the new system and exposing the old-time vice of the capitalists. How the Americans exploited the rich natural resources of his dear country by unloading casks of California wine to the royal officials, who as a result got so drunk that they could only keep one eye open, while American helicopters smuggled mountains of ores out of the country, right under the half-open eyes of the snoring drunkards.

Fong Mun stood listening. His former geography lessons had taught him that Laos, one of the world's poorest nations, had nothing to recommend itself except rain and floods. What ore? What mineral resources? The country had always lacked prerequisites such as iron, copper, zinc, and aluminum to pull it from the swamp of backwardness.

"Our country so disemboweled!" the principal lamented. "Our country is poor because the cunning Americans have stolen all the natural resources. I've seen ruins of excavation sites. I've seen crates shipped out. Only communism can heal the wounds of our country. Time to wake up, my beloved countrymen!"

The sun aligned itself above the flagpole.

The much affected principal paused a moment to wipe the sweat off his forehead with the back of his hand. "The love for our country is thicker than blood. Every one of you knows. So repeat these words loudly—with passion! Shout them out! Sing them! Live them!" He pounded his fist in the air. "Long live our country!"

"Long live our country!" the students roared.

"Down with our enemies!"

"Down with our enemies!"

As he stood in the sun, Fong Mun felt stirred. He felt like protesting against the caveman principal, who lacked poise, the suave demeanor of the learned and wise, who had no degrees to back up his title. Fong Mun's blood boiled. He wanted to shout, to brandish his fists, to denounce the fraud who had become the principal just because the Communists had come into power.

The red-faced principal saw he had succeeded in agitating the students. He would channel their agitation to action, as planned. A bright light—the light of liberation?—shone in his eyes. Without it he wouldn't be standing at the podium. He would have remained a caveman, forever ignorant.

Fong Mun shouted along. He couldn't see the principal's brandished fists. The group at the front formed two lines. The formation soon reached Fong Mun and he too became part of the line, which began to move forward, following the principal. The head of each class watched his classmates and teacher to make sure they shouted with fervor. They filed out of the school gate onto the street.

Fong Mun lagged behind and got in the middle of the procession so as to spare his family, if they happened to walk by, the shame of seeing him making a spectacle of himself in broad daylight.

The street was empty of cars and *sarm-law*, the three-wheel pedal cabs. The procession turned left at the Bungalow, moving toward the mini-park in an island of the street. Shaped like a teardrop, the park consisted of a few benches around the statue of a costumed dancer wringing a long jet of water from her waist-long black hair. The water had stopped flowing from the hair.

The procession marched past the dancer. A long block later, the principal led the way to the soccer stadium—but not into the shady spectator stand. The school filed down the slope toward the field.

There was no fence or wall, and no goal for the sport. Across from the entrance and the spectator stand, the stadium adjoined Thut Luang, a temple built by the Indian missionaries in the third century. Except for some patchy, much-trampled dry grass, the stadium stood empty.

The principal could shout his indictment and love as passionately as he wished. "Keep shouting! Let's keep it up!" he ordered his students and teachers.

They repeated the slogans.

After what seemed like an hour or so, other schools appeared at the entrance and filed down the slope toward the center.

They began to march around the stadium. Each school held up a banner, hollered slogans, kicked up dust, trampled on plastic bags and scraps of paper along the way. Fong Mun's principal, his eyes bulging, his mouth parted, sweating and panting, kept swinging his fist and yelling his idea of leadership.

These rallies at the stadium soon became a regular

event. Fong Mun's school was always the first to arrive and the last to leave.

The dinner table at home overflowed with food. Steamed spareribs. Steamed fish.

Fong Mun turned around to throw a fish bone to Auntie K.'s cats, but saw no cat under the table. He looked across the yard and saw, through her open door, Auntie K.'s three cats playing inside her hut.

He gathered the fish bones in his bowl and went to the yard. He called *meow, meow,* but no cat scurried down the hut toward him. He meowed some more. "If you don't come I'll throw the bones in the trash." He knew they were listening. Still no response. "Don't you come later and turn the trash upside down and inside out." He gave the last warning and scraped the contents of the bowl into the trash can.

Just then Auntie K. stepped down her hut with a bowl in one hand, her other hand pulling her sarong above her ankles. She crossed the courtyard and stopped under the canopy of the *mayom* tree, near the dinner table.

"Auntie K., have you had dinner?" Ahma asked.

Auntie K. said she had, although she might not have had any. She mentioned the Brothers. The wind swept the fallen *mayom* leaves. They brushed past her feet in a small whirlwind.

"They wrote down the guava tree, the old pomegranate, the sugar cane, the kafir limes, everything, even the little bush of *pandan* growing by the old clay jug. How much can a few *pandan* leaves be worth?

They have been here for years." Auntie K. pointed at her plants and spat on the ground.

Ahma pointed at the *mayom* tree with her chopsticks. "They wrote it down."

"Tell me the use." Auntie K. shook her head.

"They wrote down everything, even the coconut trees," Ahma said. "I remember when we first moved here, that tree in the back was still small." She pointed at the short coconut tree that Uncle K. had climbed. "Now it's taller than the bathing stall."

Auntie K. turned around to look, then sighed. "My boys' father planted it."

"From now on all the trees will belong to them," Ahma said, as she shoved some rice from the bowl in her hand to her mouth with the chopsticks.

"Why dwell on it?" Mr. Fong interjected.

"Isn't it right? What I just said?" Ahma threw him a glance.

"No more of this. Eat now. Eat."

Ahma scowled.

"Eat your food!" He pointed at her bowl with his chopsticks.

Ahma chewed.

Auntie K. stood around, undecided whether to stay on; then she returned to her hut.

Everyone ate without talking. When she spoke again, Ahma's voice sounded choked. "I can't even say anything now," talking as she chewed.

She slammed down the bowl. She left the table and went into her room. Her voice came through the window, "Now I can't even say a word, can't say a thing in my own home."

Mr. Fong kept eating. So did Mr. Woo, the photographer. Mrs. Fong reached for the soup with her spoon. Fong Mun heard a mosquito come close and then, through the window, Ahma's voice again.

"You think I'm too old, a burden for you, huh? Let me die, then."

Mr. Fong put down his bowl and stood up. His voice rose after hers.

After dinner—after she had calmed down—Ahma put leftovers back into pots and plates and stored them in the kitchen cabinet while Mrs. Fong put the bowls in a basin by the bathing stall.

Auntie K. crossed the courtyard again and followed Ahma into the kitchen. From within the kitchen Ahma's hand reached for the door and pulled it closed.

"A bunch of country bumpkins," Auntie K. chuckled. "They don't know a thing."

"They're all over the town now." Ahma lowered her voice. "I heard they'd ruined the building over there. They dirtied the whole place."

"Everyone knows they don't know how to use the toilet."

"They're so dull. I bet they're too lazy to clean up the place."

"They've never used a toilet, so when they see one they don't know what to do."

"You don't find a toilet in the caves."

"They ruined the language building. They shit

next to the toilet bowl, on the floor." Auntie K. chuckled.

"Such a nice building, too." Ahma sounded indignant.

"The Americans took good care of it," Auntie K. whispered. "The students did all this. Without them the Brothers would still live in the mountains."

"Forever in the caves."

"Everyone knows the students wouldn't have fired up without the signal from the Russians," Auntie K. whispered. "Did the protest that day have the power of the sea?"

"Very much like a tidal wave." Ahma nodded. "It rose above the tallest coconut tree."

The whispers stopped. Near silence. And then Auntie K. spoke again, "These cavemen have never seen a three-story building in their lives."

"They lived all their lives in the caves, so of course they'd never seen it."

"Surely the building is not a cave."

"To them it is."

They paused.

"Sometimes I'm too tired to move around," Auntie K. said. "Don't feel like dragging my old bones to the stall to soak the rice or start a fire. I take to my bed."

Then Ahma's voice burst out, as if she had finally cleared her throat. "Oh, take this, take this."

The door opened. Auntie K. stepped out with two bowls in her hands. She walked through the courtyard past the chicken coop. The disgruntled hens crooned with loud protest as a rooster pecked at them. "Always fighting!" She bent down to peer inside the coop and listen for more evidence of disharmony. "Now quiet down, go to sleep," she admonished the chickens. She stood upright and continued on to her hut.

After dinner, at seven, Fong Mun left for school.

When he returned home at nine, his mother, who sat knitting the orange sweater in an armchair, asked him what he had learned. She herself had attended two night seminars designed for housewives. "I've made some progress in my Lao vocabulary," he told her, "and I like arithmetic and botany."

She stopped knitting, appeared thoughtful.

In reality Fong Mun hardly learned anything. As a reformer, the principal advocated political education through marches, rallies, and night seminars, which replaced botany and readings of Hindu epics. Rallies in the morning and seminars at night became the curriculum. What the principal repeated in the seminars eluded Fong Mun, though, and the mindless repetition of "Marx Lenin" while denouncing the venom of capitalism made him yawn.

Would he rather take singing lessons?

At that time songs of patriotism replaced the melodies of love and folk songs as the most popular form of music among the revolutionaries-cum-students. The government broadcast the patriotic songs everywhere in town, through bull horns attached to light poles along the streets, and on the roof of a house at every street intersection, to instill a new sense of national pride in the citizenry. The singing filled the town for an hour at seven in the morning, at noon, and then at six in the evening: all free of charge.

To further awaken those who still indulged in Buddhism, the government affixed two extra-large bullhorns outside each temple, below the eaves. The frequent broadcasts made it impossible for the monks and nuns to meditate on impermanence. Distracted by the constant reminder of patriotism, they were forced to forsake the solace and peace of the cloister, return to secular life, grow their hair, pick up hoes to till the rice field.

Fong Mun learned the songs not only to enjoy the fresh tunes composed by the Vietnamese Brothers in Hanoi but also to improve his Laotian vocabulary. Through these songs he learned how hard the caveman principal had struggled for the day when music became egalitarian in the ancient royal capital called Luang Prabang.

The planning committee in the caves, with the help of Hanoi, failed to foresee another effect produced by the egalitarian music: after the broadcast one morning, a dusty silence fell on the town. No one understood why.

The committee arrested the broadcaster, interrogated him, flogged him, peeled off his nails, but failed to extract any solid confessions. The committee dispatched the half-dead broadcaster to the re-education camp.

Silence took over the town.

One day, a monk, who had been a French scholar

well versed in the Buddhist scripture but was now re-
formed by proletarian thinking, broke the dusty silence
with a revelation: the birds had stopped singing. It was
so simple and obvious that no one had thought of it.
The patriotic songs composed by the Brothers in
Hanoi were so melodious that as the sparrows listened,
they forgot to chirp—even after the songs ended. The
birds forgot to twitter and became mute. Transported,
the roosters too stopped crowing, the ducks stopped
quacking, the cicadas stopped buzzing, the clocks
stopped ticking—until the monk with common sense
broke the spell of patriotism.

The silence didn't bother Mrs. Fong. She only ob-
jected to her son's amusing himself with humming
Communist songs. Unlike Ahma, for whom education
consisted solely of book learning, Mrs. Fong used to
take her son to singing lessons. When his school hour
extended to nighttime, she knew it had changed from
a forum for scholarly inquiry to a training ground for
young revolutionaries. She probed her son about what
he had learned.

If only his family knew how he spent his school
hour, going to rallies in the morning and seminars at
night, Fong Mun thought, as he answered his mother's
question. If only she knew what went on at the seminars, and what his fanatic principal had just announced.

In the dimly lit classroom—under the giddy orange light bulb—the principal's lecture had escaped
Fong Mun's attention. Sitting in the back, he was steal-
ing a glance at Boontong in the front row when the
principal's announcement jolted him from his seat: all

needed to report to the stadium by five-thirty the next morning for the rally.

Fong Mun gaped.

"I have to go to school early." Fong Mun told Ahma to wake him up at four-thirty. They lay down and closed their eyes.

Because she herself always got up around that time, awakened by her own internal alarm clock, Ahma didn't ask why the school kept such irregular hours. Also, at that moment her attention was distracted by a rodent's screech below her bed.

"The rats are so bold now." She sat up.

Fong Mun opened his eyes. No sooner did Ahma speak than something darted along the foot of the wall from one corner to the other, under the bed.

"A fat rat," Ahma grumbled.

"Did you hear that?" he called from his bed over the partition to his mother in the next room.

"Go to sleep," his mother called back.

"Did you hear that, Mama?"

"Hush! Go to sleep."

"I thought I'd put a mousetrap under the bed already." He turned to Ahma.

"The rats are bigger than the trap," she said.

He climbed over her legs to reach for the mosquito-net opening. "I'm going to check." He stood by the bedside and was about to part the net opening to switch on the light, when Ahma said, "Don't let in the mosquitos now."

After turning on the light, he sprawled down on

his stomach and, holding onto the edge of the bed, poked his head through the net opening and peered down. The trap was under the bed, in the same corner and at the same angle where he had left it. "These rats," he grunted.

"The cats are getting lazy," Ahma said.

He turned off the light and got back in.

"Today I saw a rat run right past the cat in the kitchen, right under the cat's eyes," Ahma told him.

"I thought cats can hear rats even in their sleep. They'll jump at them."

"That cat didn't even move," Ahma said.

"How can a cat become so dull?"

"They're getting fat."

"Useless things."

"They can't move with a full stomach. And they've become picky, too. They picked at the bones and then ignored most of them, letting ants crawl all over. Now they want to eat only fish and leave the bones to the ants."

Fong Mun scolded Auntie K.'s cats. "Lazy things. From now on I'll not feed them anymore. Low-down creatures!"

"What did you say?" His mother's stern voice from the other room.

He hushed.

A second later Ahma said, "A mosquito."

He listened for the sound. He heard it come close, straight to his ears. He got ready to slap but it trailed off. "Where has it gone?" Hardly had he finished speaking than it returned. But off it flew again. Then he heard a sharp clap.

"I think I've missed it," Ahma said.

Sure enough, the buzzing sound returned a second later, and no sooner did Fong Mun hear it than he hastened to clap. His palms smarting, again he heard the buzz, like a needle drilling his eardrum.

Ahma reached for the light switch and, through the net, flipped on the light. With both the sound and the light, they spotted the mosquito on its solo hunt. Fong Mun hastened after it and clapped, but missed. It made a turn and flew over his face—a dark dot aiming at his eyelids. He felt it land on his cheek. He stayed still as he got ready to slap. Just as he raised his hand he felt a sting. He slapped his cheek. In his palm was a red dot, and in it, a dark, blurred mass.

He tossed and turned, sleeping fitfully. When Ahma woke him up he looked at the round clock on the bookcase: four-thirty. He climbed out of bed.

Ahma had heated up a pot of water for him to wash his face. As he brushed his teeth by the ditch, he saw on the street students already heading in one direction, toward the market or the stadium, though it was still dark.

At the predawn hour of five, Fong Mun left home for the stadium. He might run into wandering spirits. He shuffled boldly on the sleeping street. Here and there, in twos or threes, students in uniforms headed in the same direction. He turned at a street corner.

When he arrived, he found where his school had

convened right away: the only school in the whole dark empty stadium. He found none of the students he had seen earlier (judging by their uniforms).

The teacher for each class called roll. Everyone was present. After the roll call, the students stood waiting. Boontong stood by, hands behind his back and legs apart, watchful, aloof as usual.

As the sky began to turn gray, dim figures began gathering in the stadium. So other schools were coming for the rally, after all.

More students arrived, filling the stadium. School banners hung motionless as all stood waiting. By sunrise the largest assembly came into formation.

Fong Mun should have left home at seven or even eight, since at that hour students from the other schools were still arriving, filing in without hurry down the slope to the stadium. No doubt his principal was the only one who had ordered his school to meet there at the ghostly hour of five-thirty. The principals of other schools were more reasonable. Fong Mun's blood boiled. The heated urge to protest and scream took possession of him.

Just then a flutter of dark specks burst from the plumeria and tall bodhi treetops within the white-plastered walls of Thut Luang, up the slope along the length of the stadium. The assembly turned to look. The cluster of dark dots soared and spread out like an open fan in the cloudless sky.

At the same instant the chirping of sparrows and the fluttering of a thousand wings came within earshot. The bird cries grew louder. The army of sparrows arrived, and it looked as if they would swoop to the ground level when in the next instant they veered and shot higher—as if sucked—into the sky, turning it dark. They flew higher and farther away, into the mountains.

Another army of birds, mostly sparrows, flew over the stadium along the same path and in a blink were kilometers away.

For the next half hour or so, the assembly, gasping, witnessed the only bird exodus ever in the history of the Kingdom. Not only the sparrows that lived under the eaves but also birds of different sizes and shapes, birds that even the elders well-versed in Sanskrit and French failed to name, flew overhead, along the same path with great flutter. Green birds, red birds, a giant bird with white plumage and long slender legs, squeaked over the stadium.

After the birds flew away, the principal, ears temporarily numb, checked his watch. He disappeared in the crowd and reappeared at the front holding a bullhorn. He cried out the slogans. "Away with corruption!" "Down with the imposter!" Upon which the schools raised their flags and shouted after him. Thousands of mouths moved. He looked about him and gave the signal.

Boontong cut through the lines to flank the principal.

The school closest to the entrance began to file out, brandishing pickets and fists, up the slope to the street.

The principal, flanked by his squad of revolutionaries, pressed his school to shout more loudly. But no matter how loud they shouted, the principal remained the loudest.

The next school quickly followed the first one, and other schools began to position themselves in quick succession. Fong Mun's was the last one to file out. The time was nine-thirty.

The wave of shouts reached the market. A Vietnamese *pho* vendor at the market was too preoccupied with what she had seen earlier, the sky darkened with wings, a rare sight, to give the student demonstration another thought. She went on serving her customers.

Among the customers sat Ahma, who also bore witness to a swarm of butterflies passing the market from all directions. Butterflies with bright yellow wings and black patterns, some with inky purple wings, or orange wings—they abandoned their homes from within all corners of the ancient royal capital and headed off in the same direction as the birds.

As they fluttered past the market, over the tents and roofs, the butterflies confounded the senses of the townspeople. Overhead, the bird flight continued. So that fifteen minutes later, when the student procession marched past the street a block down from the market, the people in the market were still too dazed to notice. They didn't even blink.

But even if they had noticed, would they have obstructed the marchers? Would they have diverted their sons and daughters from their course?

The student procession passed the fountain, the

Bungalow at the intersection, the Queen's Cinema, and the New Temple and reached the Royal Palace before the entrance to Chinatown: all on one long street. The palace took up the whole block, surrounded by white-plastered brick walls.

More schools began to arrive and fill the street in front of the palace gate.

The red sentry booth by the gate stood empty. Behind the gate two rows of tall palm trees, with a passage in the middle, led to the palace's front steps, which led to the closed front door, richly decorated with gold-leaf carving. High above it, on the roof, stood the engraving of three elephants, the symbol of Lan Xan, the Kingdom of a Million Elephants: the one in the middle provided the front view, the other two, at its right and left, the side view, their long noses hanging down.

The hoarse, overheated students outside the gate would have welcomed a respite, but the ever persistent principal kept up the momentum by roaring into the bullhorn. A fire went wild in the cave of his eyes.

"Down with the king!" The shouts mounted the walls, reaching for the inner quarters of the palace.

In the royal kitchen, the royal chef, clutching the window bars, turned to his wife. "They are here!"

Wringing her hands, she looked to her husband more for confirmation than to ask a question. "First the Golden Buddha flew from the palace. Then the birds and butterflies . . . one after the other, these winged sapient beings . . ." Tears filled her eyes.

Prabang, the Golden Buddha, was reported to have disappeared from the palace. The desertion boded ill for the fate of Luang Prabang, home for heavenly beings, the ancient Buddhist capital that was named after the Golden Buddha. The certainty that the end of the Kingdom would arrive any day soon weighed on the minds of sages and peasants alike.

"I told you this would happen when the Golden Buddha flew away," the chef told his wife.

The old couple had served the king and the queen for years, preparing dishes to please the royal palate. As the old couple paced behind the kitchen window, a painful growl louder than the shouts outside the palace came from the inner quarters of the palace. At the same time a quake ripped through the kitchen. The frightened old couple, still dazed, looked to the end of the hallway to find a royal page running to them.

"The elephant, the elephant!" the boy cried breathlessly. The old chef turned around, his mouth open. "The elephant!" The threesome hurried to the rear wing, the house of the royal elephant.

A pillar in the rear wing had been broken. By the broken pillar the royal elephant had collapsed on its side in a pool of blood, its belly heaving, one tusk broken off and blood squirting from the wound. A strong, rusty, metallic odor filled the area.

"He smashed his head on the pillar." The boy's voice trembled.

The old couple moved toward the elephant and kneeled down. The tearful wife reached out one hand to close the eyes of the royal elephant. The shouts outside the palace became louder, demanding that the king step down from the throne. The old couple eyed each other. Tears rolled down their cheeks.

"The negotiation will be a peaceful one!" Boontong spoke in a thundering voice outside the gate. "We bring no arms. We don't intend to use violence." He smelled something strange, but dismissed it, sticking instead to his purpose. "But we'll wait here until the king agrees to talk."

Cheers from the students.

"This is a Bloodless Revolution," the principal called through the bullhorn. "We will wait for the king. Patiently." And then the principal sucked his breath, surprised by a sharp odor he had just inhaled.

The rusty metallic stink spread over the street and caused all to cover their noses.

More students packed into the street. They scrambled over the turf at the foot of the Golden Pagoda Mountain facing the palace, and climbed up the plumeria trees, now devoid of birds and butterflies drawn to the fragrance. Still more students surged up the flight of stairs that led to the top of the mountain, to see what went on behind the palace gate.

A student leader in front of the gate cried that the king had shown up. A wave of applause moved through the crowd.

"The king agrees to draw a pact," someone yelled.

At the summit of the Golden Pagoda Mountain, by the cloud-piercing stupa, the old monks hurried to gather at the railing to watch—down the hill full of plumeria trees—the masses blocking the street and the front of the palace at the entrance to Chinatown. The palace looked peaceful compared to the commotion outside the gate. Except for a jeep in the middle of the passage that led to the palace steps, everything looked the same as it did decades before. Behind the palace, over the wall, the brown Mekong flowed from China and Burma, on its way to Thailand, Cambodia, Vietnam, out to the South China Sea. Beyond the palace, on the opposite shore, green hillocks undulated.

A few figures stood around the jeep. No page running inside or outside the building or across the yard; no shuffling of feet along the corridors; no positioning of cannons toward the jeep or the street; no tanks.

The old monks couldn't tell whether one of the figures standing by the jeep was the king or the prime minister, because tears had filled their eyes.

The students at the base of the mountain and those standing astride the antler branches of the plumeria trees couldn't tell which figure was the king, either, but not because tears had filled their eyes.

"That one." A student pointed.

"No, no. The king's in the jeep."

"No. The one wearing glasses is the king."

"Have you ever seen the king wearing glasses?"

"Then who is carrying on the negotiation by the jeep?"

Fong Mun stretched his neck to look. The closest he had ever come to the king was when at the beginning of movies the audience stood up to salute the king as his picture flashed on the screen and the national anthem played. When the royal retinue passed his home, Fong Mun had never been able to spot the king in the motorcade.

Now Fong Mun hid in the back, on the turf under a plumeria tree, waiting. He had lost sight of the principal and Boontong in the masses outside the palace gate.

The gate opened just enough to allow someone in. The two students on the plumeria trunk still argued over who they thought the king was. A year ago, all these students had saluted the king's portrait with great reverence. Today, they wouldn't leave until the king stepped from the throne. They would not leave even if their principals told them to go home for lunch.

Fong Mun waited.

Just then sunlight disappeared. Fong Mun looked up. The sky was clear, but a patch of shadow had moved—and was moving—over the sun. As the shadow gnawed away at the sun, darkness fell over the town, and Fong Mun's waiting was over.

He scurried down the hill onto the street, sidled through the crowd of students. It got darker. While trying to appear calm and act fast, he squeezed his way through the crowd. It became completely dark. He stopped and had to wait again, frantic, silently willing the eclipse to be over.

The eclipse seemed to have stirred the crowd to even greater frenzy. The shouting took on mountainous proportions as the shadow swallowed the sun.

Gnawing. Swallowing. Then the shadow spat out a bit of the sun, and light emerged. As it became lighter, Fong Mun began to move. He hurried past the new Temple toward the Queen's Cinema. The shadow moving away. More light. He hurried past the cinema and turned left at the intersection, and as he passed his own school, he paused to look. He would not go back there again. More and more light.

The market stood in plain view. The *pho* vendor got ready to close her noodle stand for the day. Outside the market, on the street, the *sarm-law* drivers leaned on their vehicles, still idly smoking hand-rolled cigarettes, still waiting for customers.

Fong Mun rushed along, his heart pounding wildly.

At home, Ahma set the lunch table. The Fongs sat down to dine. No customers in the shop. No traffic on the street. No pedestrians on the sidewalk. No sound of tableware clanking as the Fongs ate. No one spoke. Auntie K.'s three cats slept with full bellies by the door of her hut, where sunlight caressed them. The sunlight felt different after the eclipse, as if it had been yanked upside down. It felt weak, ashen, bled. A rat darted across the cats' faces. Unperturbed, the cats slept on.

"I almost forgot about the episode of the botany teacher's wedding until after some time in Bangkok, when I got homesick and craved the coconut-chili-peanut fish soup." Fong Mun rested the side of his face on one hand, his elbow propped on the armrest of the sofa. "And in America too, thinking about it makes me hungry." A sigh. "Even now."

"Restaurants don't serve the dish?"

Fong Mun peered at Raymond. The naivete of a beautiful man will always be forgiven. "No. I'd have to make it from scratch. I've picked up the best recipes in the most unexpected places."

"You mentioned Bangkok."

"Yes. Soon after the king's dethronement I dropped out of school and went to Bangkok. I felt cheated. All the lectures and assemblies turned out to be a rehearsal for the coup. Guess what—after he achieved his scheme, the school principal had no more uses for the daily rallies. So he sent the students to work in the rice fields."

"What about Boontong?" Raymond asked.

"The Blessed Copper? He noticed I'd stolen glances at him. He looked disgusted. His eyes became steel. Never looked at me."

"Straight boys. They're heartless."

Tell me about it. Fong Mun's mouth puckered. "He reserved his attention for girls."

"If only he'd known what was on your mind!"

"I'd have gotten in trouble."

"What would he have done? Strangled you?"

"Probably." Fong Mun crossed his legs. "I didn't think I would see him again. But I ran into him two years later in a refugee camp—now seeking resettlement in the Western world, for freedom and democracy!"

"The revolutionary?"

"Darker than before, more good-looking. He waited with two girls for a bus to go downtown. He wore an Adidas T-shirt, an unbuttoned jean jacket, a pair of jeans, a silver amulet necklace for luck, a watch on his right wrist, a silver bracelet on his left. Imagine if he ends up here, sunning himself on a California beach in a pair of Speedo trunks, upgrading his jewelry to gold!"

"Is that the way you still see him—a heart throb in a Speedo? After what he had done to his homeland?" Raymond raised his eyebrows.

Fong Mun blushed at letting himself get carried away, as if Raymond had stumbled onto his rendezvous with the Blessed Copper in the depth of the night. In which Fong Mun was a thirtysomething caterer who had gained some weight through years of food tasting, his body flabby here and there, while the body of his amour remained compact and copper-toned as twenty years before, with the silver amulet necklace resting on the bare, strong chest. Yes, he deplored all that the Blessed Copper stood for, but the pair of ghostly swimming trunks still hung in his head.

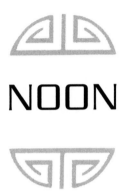

NOON

1995, San Francisco, California

They soaked two small bundles of bean threads, cracked an egg in a large bowl, added salt and black pepper—plenty of black pepper, to enhance the aroma.

As he heated a pot of water to boil a package of rice noodles, Fong Mun told Raymond, "People prefer egg rolls to salad and noodles."

"We all know the virtue of eating more vegetables."

"I don't see why they don't use the opportunity. They keep diving for the plate of egg rolls and ignore the tray of noodles and raw vegetables. So I dispense with them. I stop making fresh noodles. Saves time. And the salad, which calls for at least three kinds of vegetables, only clutters the kitchen table and my attention." Fong Mun turned toward the stove to lower the heat and proceeded to soak the package of rice noodles in the pot of hot water. "This way I can focus just on making the egg roll." Fong Mun peered at Raymond. "It becomes an appetizer."

Raymond said, "I have all the confidence it can serve as the main dish by itself. Your guests have proved it on the dinner table, and they'll continue to do so."

Umm. Sure to have a sweet tongue, to please the soft spot of my ears. Fong Mun drained the noodles in a colander.

After he mixed the ingredients, he showed Raymond how to wrap. He folded one corner of the wrapper, like a dog ear, over the contents, then rolled once, keeping the shape tight and compact, folded the two corners at the right and the left over the contents, continued rolling until reaching the final corner. He sealed it with some egg white.

Raymond put some of the filling near a corner of a wrapper, folded it like a dog ear, rolled, and folded the other two corners of the wrapper over, rolling and trying to shape it.

"You should have told the lawyer the shape is crucial too, not just the frying," Raymond said. "You call this egg roll?" He held it up.

They burst out laughing.

"It's a wallet! What did you do to it?"

"Well, you saw me. I followed what you did. I rolled," Raymond said.

They laughed. The poor misshapen egg roll fell apart in Raymond's hand.

"Try again."

After wrapping, Fong Mun opened the windows

and heated up the wok, to which he added some oil. As he watched Raymond put the egg rolls in one by one, so close to him, he pulled Raymond into his arms.

They stayed that way for a minute. They didn't hear the egg rolls sizzling. "Raymond . . ." They held tighter together. Raymond squeezed Fong Mun's arm. They looked into each other's eyes, and when they moved close, about to kiss, they smelled burning food.

"Watch out." Fong Mun hurried to flip the burning egg rolls with a pair of chopsticks.

Raymond laughed. "Well, maybe our lawyer friend is right after all. Frying does account for the quality."

Fong Mun turned off the stove, removed the burned egg rolls, reheated the wok, and put another batch in. This time they fried the egg rolls to a uniform gold.

Raymond clucked his tongue.

Fong Mun laid a piece of paper towel on a plate and placed the egg rolls there. He cut some to small pieces with a pair of scissors, put the plate on the table. He showed Raymond how to make the sauce: mix equal amounts of water, sugar, vinegar, and fish sauce, add some chopped garlic and chili paste.

"Now you know." Saying this, Fong Mun put the bowl of sauce on the table. He had shown Raymond all the steps. It was now up to Raymond to learn them by heart, without the assistance of a recipe.

For the meal they included vegetables: red leaf lettuce, mint, cilantro, other herbs, and even a star fruit. When Ahma ate egg roll, she had cut open a star fruit and added a slice to the leaf of the pouchlike red leaf lettuce in her hand.

After they sat down, Fong Mun prompted Raymond to start. As Raymond took a leaf of lettuce from the plate, Fong Mun fetched a piece of egg roll with a pair of chopsticks and lowered it—across the table—into the lettuce in Raymond's hand. Raymond nodded slightly, with a grin, the eye contact imparting his thank-you. And Fong Mun's chopsticks reached for the noodles. Again he lowered them into the leaf of lettuce in Raymond's hand. Raymond smiled slightly and reached for some cilantro and mint. He then wrapped the leaf of lettuce and dipped it in the sauce. Just the way Ahma had served the dish. Fong Mun felt contented, watching Raymond eat.

"So you came up with the recipes through memory." Raymond munched with gusto.

"Through memory and through trial and error."

"That's how you wrote the cookbook!" Raymond exclaimed as he again dipped the pouch of food in the sauce.

"In some cases I remember the steps so well the cooking is foolproof. The *jong* serve the best example—"

"The Chinese tamale?"

"Is that how you call it?" Fong Mun laughed. "Back in Laos, my family made them for New Year. Took almost a whole day just to boil them. I craved them so much during the first few years in California—one time I decided to make some for a New Year potluck. I went to Oakland Chinatown but I couldn't find fresh *jong* leaves, only the dry, ancient-looking ti leaves wrapped in dusty plastic bags.''

With the ingredients snugly in the front seat, he had driven to Oakland Hills, to the house of a member of his Asian men's group. It had been his idea, to make *jongs* for the potluck. He arrived early to cook, since he knew from experience that the *jong* needed to boil for several hours. The host led him into the kitchen.

"I soaked the glutinous rice and the mung beans, before I marinated the lean pork flanks. I boiled the *jong* in a pot. They were cooked in two hours. So flavorful." Fong Mun let out an uh of satisfaction.

"That's because you hadn't eaten them for so long." Raymond took another mouthful of the egg roll.

Fong Mun had surveyed the guests at the potluck, the takeout food they brought. Although he had been in the men's group for a year, he felt unable to relate to the members there. It had to do with his spoken English, his speech having to go through a rougher curvature of words, which slowed down his thoughts, blanched his wits, tied up his vocal cords, stumped his mouth. So that he found his experience with the group as unexciting and impersonal as the takeout food the group brought to the potluck. They didn't know much about him—about why, for example, he took such pains to prepare the *jong*. But of course it was not their tradition, in California, to prepare *jong* from scratch to celebrate lunar New Year. The result didn't warrant the time and the labor involved. At the potluck, he didn't touch the potstickers and the chicken salad, but savored the *jongs*.

Watching Raymond now, Fong Mun spoke. "Nowadays Chinatown sells them all year round—in different variations, too. The lunar New Year seems so dead here. People go to work on New Year's day! After work they go home and have their own New Year's dinner. Back then, back in Laos, we gathered in school for the annual event. Everyone knew each other."

Raymond took another piece of egg roll. "Wasn't there a war?"

"It went on for years, even before I was born, and lasted through my boyhood. The fight between the royal army and the Lao Conq—the same Brothers who loved to have their photos taken but never got the chance until they won the war—the fight took place at night. It lasted as long as my toothache." Fong Mun sucked his teeth, the way he had done in his boyhood to momentarily dull the ache.

The chronic toothache occurred only at night. It afflicted not only Fong Mun but the entire population of Luang Prabang: the peasants, the monks and the nuns, the royal families. Spasms of pain coincided with the sound of machine guns and cannons from the outskirts of town. But for the curfew the whole town would have flocked to the dentist and banged at his door. Of course, the dentist also huddled in his home, wide awake like everyone else, suffering from the epidemic toothache.

Spasms of pain kept the whole town awake, and

yet the town appeared so still, as if it had been evacuated, or was in deep slumber, submerged in complete darkness (no one was allowed to turn on a light or light a candle), oblivious to flashes of bright orange fire and smoke flaring up in the countryside, near the airport. On several occasions the Brothers had advanced quite close, only a few kilometers from the heart of town, but the royal army managed to fight them off.

"The cannons shook our house. In the daytime helicopters flew over our roof and dropped off wounded soldiers at the hospital. Anesthetic was in short supply. So the dentist had to pull teeth the primitive way, saving the anesthetic for the wounded soldiers."

The Brothers occupied the northern part of Luang Prabang, up the Mekong River, caves and historical sites that housed beautiful statues of Buddha. The Brothers slept in the daytime and returned to attack at night. The highland traders on their way to town or on their way back to the mountains were often ambushed as well. Land mines were planted by both the royal army and the Brothers.

"So the toothache lasted for years, throughout the early seventies. New Year's and festivals became the anesthetic."

February 1973, Luang Prabang, Laos

Ahma laid three large, long leaves in front of her on the table.

These deep green leaves had an oily sheen. They looked like banana leaves but were narrower, sturdier, stiffer, greener. The highlanders, the Hmongs, sold them in the lowlands once a year, shortly before the lunar New Year, to the Chinese and the Vietnamese for use as *jong* wrappers.

The plant remained little known to the lowlanders. Did it have the shape of a banana tree, since its leaves resembled banana leaves? Was it a bird of paradise gone wild and gigantic, except that the highlanders had trimmed it, thus tamed it? Castrating the plant the way they castrated roosters and turned them into capons? The plant grew no blossom or fruits. The lowlanders saw the highlanders arrive with a truckload of chickens and ducks, bundles of firewood, bags of tobacco, and stacks of these long leaves they had no name for, although they recognized them.

Just like a cut-open fish belly, Ahma thought, as she spread a bowl of rice along the midsection of the leaf. The image of the Green Fishtail beset by spiderwebs and rusting in the garage came to her. When the townspeople saw Ahma and her son first arrive in town in this American car in the mid-1950s, they named it the Green Fishtail, because its sides looked like fish fins. The trip from the capital to Luang Prabang took one day. When they reached the ancient Buddhist sanctuary, the birds disappeared into eaves of houses, the canopy of trees, and the neighboring hillsides; and the butterflies rested their wings under the branches of the plumeria trees; and flowers bloomed in unison, gardenias, tuberoses, wild orchids; and the elephants came out from the palace grounds to dance in the street. However, the human newcomers found themselves without homes, unable to speak the language, and with empty stomachs.

On top of the layer of rice Ahma now added a bowl of mung beans that she had soaked overnight and decoated. She put a strip of pork on top, then added another bowl of mung beans to cover the pork, and finally, another bowl of rice to complete the coating. She then rolled up the *jong* and tied it with two long bamboo strings. Each *jong* had the circumference of a rice bowl, the length of an arm.

She made *jong* every lunar New Year. Over the years the family had increased from two members (she and her son) to three (add a daughter-in-law), then four (plus a grandson). And each year Ahma increased the amount of *jong* she made. "More mouths to feed," she explained when her daughter-in-law tried to point out that the family could not possibly eat all those *jong*. The leftovers would get moldy. Ahma turned a deaf ear and went on making *jong* because even after years in Laos, she remained a refugee with an empty stomach.

Now, in the middle of the courtyard a young worker, nicknamed Ang, built a pit under the canopy of the *mayom* tree and the clotheslines. He set four rocks, in accordance with the four directions. On top of the rock formation he set the boiler, a gasoline tank that had been cut in half. Ahma would place the *jong* there and boil them for one day and one night. Ang shook the boiler to make sure it stayed balanced. Into each of the four openings formed by the rocks, he pushed a log, big, long logs that ensured a consistent fire.

Then Ang took his bicycle and went home.

At dinner time, Ahma cleared the table.

The wrapping continued after dinner. Ahma's Vietnamese friends came to help. They gathered at the table and knew what to do. They laid down the leaves on the table, dug the bowl into the tray of rice. They worked rapidly, wrapping the *jong* all in uniform size. Such skillful hands. They fought off drowsiness by chatting.

They finished at ten. They had worked so hard

they were ready for bed. Ahma stored the *jong* in the kitchen.

At four the next morning, Ahma flung open the side door, stepped into the walkway, and startled the wandering spirits that gathered around the empty boiler and blew icy breaths.

Just then the sound of a bicycle came near—to Ahma it was a signal of Ang arriving. He left his bike along the wall of the darkroom where Mr. Fong developed film. When the workman saw the light in the kitchen, it signaled to him that Ahma had gotten up. He coughed, hung his hat on the hook by the post, struck a match to light a cigarette.

As Ahma flicked on the kitchen light and the workman lit his cigarette, the spirits bounced off the tank, because they did not escape hell only to be trapped again in the burning caldron sputtering with boiling water.

After taking one puff and blowing it out, Ang started work. He helped Ahma put the *jong* into the boiler and start the fire.

"What is the matter? Running in such a hurry!" Ahma turned around with the cleaver in her hand. As usual, at ten o'clock, she was chopping meat by the kitchen door.

"Capons—capons!" Fong Mun called out as he ran to her down the walkway. "The *bah-meo* arrived—they're outside already, they have capons."

Ahma wiped her hands on a towel by the chopblock. She stood up to hold his hands and the two of them went to the front of the shop.

Ahma studied the cages (knit with bamboo straws in a diagonally crisscross pattern) of capons on the sidewalk.

Unlike the roosters or hens, which would fight for a space, the crowd of capons stood idly, gazing dully through the cage without creating a fuss. Castrated roosters, the capons had lost their male aggressiveness, not bothering to fight for territory. Neither cocks nor hens, they became contented, fat, given to crouching. They fed on rice husks, eating all day.

The Hmongs from the highlands, the *bah-meo*, stood waiting for the unloading of goods.

Holding Fong Mun's hand, Ahma circled the cages. A capon happened to thrust its neck out. Ahma bent down for a closer look, to see how fat it was. Fong Mun freed his hand from Ahma's and crouched down to look too. The capon withdrew its neck from the opening and shifted its feet.

"How much will you sell that one for?" Ahma pointed, her accent heavy.

The Hmong woman turned in the direction of Ahma's finger. "Three hundred," she said in an equally heavy accent.

"That's too much. One hundred fifty." Ahma stood up and without waiting for a reply reached into her pocket.

The Hmong shook her head. "Three hundred," she insisted.

"One hundred eighty," Ahma said, determined to

haggle. She turned and walked away, her hand withdrawn from the pocket.

"Two hundred fifty. Two hundred fifty." The seller waved after Ahma.

Ahma took out her purse before she turned around and opened it. She counted the bills and gave two hundred kips to the seller.

The woman took the money and counted. She looked up. "No, not two hundred. I can't sell it for two hundred."

Ahma stood there. And then the seller, even as she protested about how a fat capon was worth more than two hundred kips, stooped down to untie the cage. The capons shifted their feet and darted their eyes in all directions. The seller unfastened the bamboo string and unwound the double helix the string had formed. She parted the cage opening and reached in for the capon Ahma had pointed at.

The capon drew away, but the seller kept extending her hand. The hand touched the belly first, and then fumbled down the belly along the thigh to the foot. The capon jumped and lifted one foot, but the hand had closed in on it and clamped it together with the other foot. As its feet came together, the capon lost balance. At that moment its world turned upside down.

Holding its feet, the seller yanked the capon from the cage. As the creature fluttered its wings in a frenzy, Ahma realized—now that she looked closer—it was not as fat as she had first thought. She felt cheated. The seller dropped the capon in an empty cage and fastened the opening briskly with a bamboo straw, for the new owner.

Ahma carried the cage inside the shop, crossed the threshold to the walkway, walked over to the court-yard, and laid the cage in a corner beside the broom stand and the chicken coop.

Fong Mun's bowl of rice noodles on the table had cooled down. "Throw it away if you don't want to eat anymore," Ahma told him.

A beggar came in the front door.

Ahma followed Fong Mun's eyes. The beggar crouched by the display counter, below which was the cash drawer. "They come awfully early. Endless bother." She looked away. "Give her ten kips from the drawer."

The beggar kept both of her hands raised above her head as she waited to receive alms, sure of and ready for it. Her body shook uncontrollably, rocked with a vibration: her jaw, her mouth, her hands, her thighs, her knees, and her pelvic area shook, as if she were crouching on a springboard. She was a leper, the crazy woman who lived in the mortuary in the back of the hospital across from his school.

Fong Mun took a ten-kip bill from the cash drawer under the counter and went to give it to the beggar. He stopped two feet away from her and handed the money over. Ahma had warned him not to come too close to a leper. The brush of a leper's sleeves on the door frame could leave germs that would rot the fin-gers, the palms, the forearms, of whoever happened to lean on the door.

* * *

The Fongs closed the shop for New Year but kept a door open for those customers who came in to pick up their photos.

At noon a group of Hmongs filed into the shop, young men's military boots crunching through the entrance, their rifles carried behind their backs, young women's bracelet belts and large brass neck rings, in layers, clinking and clanking.

They gathered in front of the counter to view the photos on display, pointed to those they liked, and chattered with loud abandon and mirth.

Ahma was adding more firewood to boil the *jong* when the Hmongs stepped in. She immediately went indoors. "The shop is closed. Come back after New Year," she told them in her usual loud voice and heavy accent.

They glanced up, eyed her blankly, and ignored her by continuing to talk among themselves and pointing at the enlarged photo of the winner of the beauty contest in the glass showcase. Her long bare neck, her smile. In the framed enlargement, the lowland beauty kept her head turned slightly sideways as she held a few strings of plastic flowers hanging from a rod under the ceiling of the studio.

Ahma stepped up closer. "I said the shop is closed. Now leave." She waved them away.

A young soldier pointed across the room to an enlargement in the showcase and pointed back at the palm-sized photo on the display counter, under the glass tabletop, for comparison. His wife smiled shyly as she lowered her neck to the counter for a closer look, enraptured by the resemblance. The husband was in town on leave from battle. And the couple wanted to have their photos taken before he returned to the fighting.

Ahma could do nothing about the unwelcome customers. She ignored the *jong* boiling in the center of the courtyard and instead sat behind the counter to guard the shop. In a better mood, she would have simply begun her meditative chant, counting the string of beads and staring past the customers as if they were nothing more than dust. But today she could only scowl at them.

The young women had decided they wanted to look like the beauty holding strings of dusty plastic flowers dangling from a rod under the ceiling, and were determined to be photographed. They found their way to the dressing room. Behind the dusty, half-parted dark red curtain, the husbands—some of them grew opium in the highlands, most were now enlisted by the United States to fight the Brothers—laid their rifles in a dark corner and took out American cigarettes and lighters, not hand-rolled cigarettes and matches. The women took out their costumes from their bags and unfolded them.

Ahma got up from the chair, took a few quick steps to the dressing room. She pulled the curtain all the way to the wall, revealing a roomful of eager customers. Her voice rose above the clink-clank of the neck rings and bracelet bells: "There's no one here. No photo master here to take pictures. How many

times have I told you? And don't touch the brush."
She snatched it from under a woman's hand.

The woman in front of the mirrors had begun dabbing some water from the tin cup to her hair and had been about to pick up the brush. Her hand in the air, the woman turned toward Ahma with her mouth open like an O. Her O disappeared as Ahma, taller and louder, outstared her.

The husbands picked up the rifles in the corner and mounted them behind their backs. The wives returned their costumes and ornaments to their cloth bags. Still chatting, all began to file out of the dressing room. They passed the counter, and as they stepped out, the men's military boots crunched, the women's bracelet bells and brass neck rings clinked and clanked. All of which grated on Ahma's nerves.

Only after these sounds dimmed and eventually vanished did Ahma return to the courtyard to tend to the firewood.

Fong Mun sat on a stool watching the firewood crackle in the pit and rubbing his palms near the fire.

A sliver of a moon hung behind the *mayom* branches. The hour when thieves became active had arrived.

The presence of the worker, Ang, whose bike leaned on the wall, reassured Fong Mun. Ang would chase or catch any thief.

The *jong* boiling—the bubbling. The firewood crackling and popping.

Ahma came to the pit. She stooped down and

pushed the burning piece of wood more into it. Only Ang or Mr. Fong was strong enough to carry these logs.

When Fong Mun got up that morning, the fire had already started. Now, past his bedtime, and the fire was still going, the *jong* boiling.

"It'll be done soon," Ahma said.

Fong Mun felt wide awake, sitting under the clear starry sky. The rustle of the wind through the banana trees and the steady, clear bubbling sound comforted him. He rubbed his palms together, absorbing the warmth of the fire, wishing this moment would last. But the moon had moved low and would disappear from sight soon, near midnight. His mother had gone to sleep. The photographer had returned and had gone to bed.

"Go to sleep now," Ahma told Fong Mun. "Don't catch cold."

"Will the *jong* be cooked soon?"

"Yes, any minute now," she said as she checked the boiler once more.

Ang sat in the long bench smoking. In front of him a red dot glowed. It moved close to his mouth.

Ahma lifted the lid. The bubbling. "Help Ahma with the flashlight," she called.

Fong Mun stood up. He took the flashlight and shone it on the boiler as Ahma turned and flipped the *jong*, poked them with a stick as if they could respond. "Almost done now," she said, and covered the bubbling boiler with the lid. On the way back to the stool, she told Ang to take a nap if he felt sleepy.

He said no and kept smoking.

"Any minute now," she told Ang. "When this last piece of wood finishes burning. You can go home soon."

Mr. Fong had not returned, still out chatting and drinking coffee with his friends. He was a social man who enjoyed spending time more with his friends than with his family. Every night, after dinner, he joined his friends.

Ahma picked up the round string of prayer beads and resumed fingering the beads and mumbling the chant. Fong Mun wondered how she learned to pray the way she did. In what language? Cantonese or Vietnamese? Not Sanskrit, surely. Fingers never idle, such was her devotion to the gods.

A chilly wind blew off the pond over the duckweeds and through the banana grove. The long banana leaves waved.

Fong Mun heard Auntie K. cough inside her hut.

When the last piece of wood ceased burning, Ahma decided the *jong* were cooked.

"If they are left in the boiler, thieves might steal them," she told Fong Mun as she removed the lid.

She and the worker carried the steamy *jong* pair by pair to the kitchen and hung them on a bamboo pole like clothes on a clothesline. The sound they made stirred the chickens in the coop.

When finished, Ang put the lid back on the boiler.

"Go home to sleep now, Ang," Ahma told him. "Let the coals cool by themselves."

Ang thumped out his cigarette, mounted his bike, and rode off down the foggy street.

Ahma locked the kitchen door and went inside the house with Fong Mun.

Ang had been young, barely seventeen or eighteen, when he started working for the Fongs, a lean lad, with thick, unkempt hair, somewhat curly, not the usual straight black hair of lowlanders. He spoke with an accent, which revealed his mountain tribe background. After a few years of working for the Fongs, he grew from a lanky lad to a sinewy man. Hard physical labor had changed him. He got married and lived on the hillside.

The Fongs didn't know Ang was missing until after New Year when he didn't show up for work. No one—not even his family—knew what had happened to him. His co-workers and friends thought the guerrillas had captured him, on that February night when he went home after work, after the last piece of firewood had finished burning and he had put away the *jong*. Pessimistic about Ang's return, his co-workers began to think that he had been shot, his body disposed of.

Perhaps, on his way home that night, he stepped on a mine planted by the Lao Cong—or by the Hmongs working for the United States.

No one found any traces of explosion or remains of the workman. His family and neighbors thought he had run into a ghost who had summoned his soul. Distressed by uncertainty, they believed he was dead and prayed for the peace of his soul.

* * *

In the late afternoon of New Year's Eve, Mrs. Fong stood in the courtyard, right outside the kitchen, and called her son over. She stooped by the cage where a rooster cowered, disturbed by human presence so close. Ahma had killed the capon and used its fat to make capon rice.

Fong Mun stood beside his mother. She opened the cage, reached inside to grab the flapping wings of the rooster. She told Fong Mun to be quick. He held Ahma's chopping knife, getting ready to kill a chicken for the first time. Mrs. Fong plucked the feathers from the throat of the struggling rooster. "Do it quick," she told him. He couldn't back out now. He crouched beside her, holding the knife.

She held the feet of the doomed rooster with one hand and grabbed its neck, pulled it back, and held it tightly against the wings with her other hand, tilting its throat over the bowl, to catch blood.

"I've never seen anyone like your grandma. One day, all the customers will be chased away by her." Mrs. Fong then ordered her son to slit the rooster's throat.

"I already did."

She peered at the bowl. "The blood barely drips. Look. Once more. Just do it quick."

The rooster got free from her hands and began a blind run, fluttering its wings and jerking its neck across the yard, under the canopy of the *mayom* tree and the clotheslines.

She pushed Fong Mun. "Catch it! Don't let it run off!"

Fong Mun didn't take the step forward.

Mrs. Fong hurried after the rooster, grabbed it. "Now hold it."

He couldn't hold the rooster. He didn't think it would put up such a fight. The beating wings of the dying chicken blinded him, scraped his arms.

Just as he let go, his mother reached for it. Holding its feet with one hand and folding its neck between its wings with the other, she told Fong Mun, "Pick up the knife!"

He slit. A red stream squirted from the throat into the bowl. Holding the weakly struggling rooster over the bowl, Mrs. Fong continued, "She doesn't like to have customers around. Why doesn't she close the shop? She can live in peace for good. I don't understand your grandmother." When the stream thinned down to drips, Mrs. Fong released the rooster, already limp.

Ahma then boiled the rooster, plucked it, to make soup out of it. Fong Mun, on his way in and out of the kitchen, excited more about New Year's Day than about the dinner, observed Ahma boiling the blood, the liver, and the heart. She soaked some bean threads, and when the soup was done and seasoned, she boiled them in there as well. She diced the coagulated blood and liver, chopped the rooster, transferred them to a plate, to be served separately. She cut some green onions to two inches in length, and some cilantro, and added them to the bowl of steamy bean-thread chicken soup. She tossed in some black pepper and served the soup.

Too excited about the raffle tomorrow and the prospect of receiving money in red envelopes to feel hungry or sit still, Fong Mun pushed the bowl of soup away from him and Ahma pushed it back in front of him, asking him to eat. He moved the bowl away again and his family had to force him to eat. He swallowed some soup. His family also forced him to eat some rice (cooked in capon fat) and the duck stewed with gingko seeds.

It would be the best New Year's Eve dinner he would ever have because it was the least appreciated at the time.

For breakfast on the New Year morning, Ahma sliced a *jong* cross-section and pan-fried the slices until they turned crispy brown. She put them on a plate, sprinkled some sugar on top.

Meanwhile Mrs. Fong had difficulty dressing Fong Mun. The tweeds irritated him. "It makes me itch all over." He squirmed.

"Do you want me to take it off? If you don't like the new suit, what will you wear?"

"The one I wore last year."

"Would you rather wear the old one?" She looked shocked.

"I would rather."

"You want to wear that old *comple't* for New Year?"

"It's more comfortable."

"You wore it last year. What's wrong with the new one? Try it on."

"It makes me itch!"

As she fetched the old coat from the closet and helped him put it on, she lectured him. "I've never seen any child like you. Everyone likes to wear new clothes. Everyone but you."

"The new one makes me itch."

"Stop talking back. The new coat looks so sharp and proper. But you never listen." She buttoned up his coat. "I'll not buy you new clothes if you don't wear them. Now put on the shoes."

He puckered his mouth tightly.

"What now? Put on the new shoes. At least you'll wear *them*?" She pointed at the pair of brown shoes.

He slipped them on. In the right pocket of his coat, he found the torn half of a raffle ticket from the year before. The year before he had gotten a soap for a prize. Although it slightly disappointed him, he'd learned to make do, content with having less. He hoped to win a bigger prize this year.

He came to the dining table.

Ahma urged him, "Eat now, else it'll cool down soon."

"I'm not hungry."

"Eat a little, eat before you go."

And so the scene of the night before repeated itself: Fong Mun told Ahma he was not hungry and pushed the food away, and she urged him to eat. What did a child know? Of course he would always choose fun over food, the playground over the kitchen. "You have to eat before you can go to the gathering. Hurry, eat and get going, it's almost eight," she told him.

After breakfast Mr. Fong put on a *comple't*. Did his wife choose the suit for him? Did she choose his shoes?

Fong Mun waited for his father by the motorcycle, to ride to school, where the celebration would take place.

Mrs. Fong chose to stay home—she didn't like crowds.

After her husband and son rode to the celebration on the motorcycle, Mrs. Fong went to the yard to cut some roses growing near the mango tree. She put the roses in a vase, filled it with sparkling water, and carried it indoors. The scent of roses followed her into the house, to the studio. The tripods for light bulbs and the camera, and the strings of plastic flowers dangling from a rod under the ceiling, were put away in a corner. She set the vase on a glass table in the spot where customers posed for the camera. On the table was a tray of red and black watermelon seeds, sweetened wintermelon slices, and fresh apples imported from Bangkok.

In the corner of the studio stood a large vase and in it was a tall branch of tiny, meager peach blossom (a traditional decoration for New Year). The part of the country unoccupied by the Pathet Lao, the peaceful part, was not cold enough for peach trees to grow. But occasionally, in early February, shortly before New Year, the highlanders would have a few bony branches of tiny peach blossom for sale.

Mrs. Fong returned to her room, took out the eye-liner, put on some makeup, fixed her hair, changed into a new dress she had designed, to transform herself once a year. She followed each step with leisure, unmoved by the prospect of the New Year celebration. She also followed each step with care, in communion with herself, to renew herself. For years she had chosen to stay home on the morning of New Year and followed her own private ritual of cutting fresh roses from the garden and making herself up.

In her new dress, she returned to the studio. All the doors and windows in the shop were closed, which kept the sunlight off and the air cool. The only source of light came from the glow of the lightbulbs and the joss sticks in the altar where images of Chinese dieties were arranged in a row. The images smiled on, emanating kindness and serenity.

Mrs. Fong sat down in the rattan chair and inhaled deeply the strong, rich scent of apples and roses blended together. Her favorite scent, that combination. A phonograph stood by the wall, but music, especially love songs, would distract her from enjoying the scent, wake her from the muteness and emptiness of the universe, remind her of—and perhaps even make her long for?—the noises of life. Ethereal smoke coiled from the joss sticks in the altar.

She picked up a slice of candied wintermelon from the tray on the table in front of her. And before lunch, before her husband returned from the noises of the celebration, she would remove the lipstick and the rest of the makeup, and trade her new dress for plain everyday wear. In this way she kept her celebration away from her family and the community.

Fong Mun and his father rode past the hospital. Toward its back stood a small one-room building, a mortuary: always dark inside, always unlit. A flight of stairs led to the doorless entrance.

As Fong Mun sat wide-legged, holding his father's waist, he turned his eyes toward the mortuary. Through the thinning fog and the dark entrance: a candle flickering in front of a body covered in a white cloth on the floor, a young Hmong woman hunched over the body, crying.

To go to school, Fong Mun had to pass the hospital. Or he could take the long route, four times as far, going around the neighborhood. When he didn't see the beggar who lived in the mortuary, he would see bodies on the floor, sometimes untended, with a lighted candle. Once he saw a large bright-red spot on the white cloth that covered the body.

There were seldom more than two or three bodies, wounded Hmong soldiers who died in the hospital. Almost always Fong Mun caught a Hmong woman crying, hunched over the dead, crying as if to dig out her heart and liver, delving still further inside herself for the source of her pain.

What made it possible to cry this way? Pain in all of its depth and breadth. Bottomless, boundless, inexhaustible pain.

Should Fong Mun not have looked death in the eye on New Year's Day, as the motorcycle passed the mortuary? No, he shouldn't have—but he was tempted. Should he have averted his eyes? Yes, he should have, for a happy occasion was now tainted by death and sorrow. To come near the mortuary on the New Year's Day, to hear such harrowing sound, to come in contact with the odor of the dead, always detectable around the confines of the mortuary, and to have it follow you: bad luck indeed. Taboo. Henceforth this would be Fong Mun's condition: to find sorrow in happiness and vice versa.

Mr. Fong did not share his son's curiosity. He did not steal a quick glance inside the mortuary. He was busy watching out for loose gravel on the bumpy road to the New Year celebration.

Mr. Fong parked by the roadside between two cars. Cars were parked alongside the school, by the ditch overgrown with weeds. Branches of bougainvillea thrust through the school fence, vying for the height of the oleander and the young betel palm trees alongside it. The gate, normally closed, stayed open to welcome the guests arriving in dark suits or bright dresses. Across the two pillars of the gate hung a red banner with words brush-painted in gold: The Thirty-sixth Annual New Year Gathering of the Lao Overseas Chinese Association in Luang Prabang.

The New Year song blared through a bullhorn used as a loudspeaker attached to each pillar. Because the song was good for only one day a year, the principal played it over and over, repeating the same congratulatory message in a happy, simple, jarring ensemble, to make up for the other 364 days.

The principal greeted the arriving guests by the gate. Normally, on a school day, he kept a stern face. But on this day he kept a smiling face as he greeted the guests with *"gong ci far chai."*

The students did not recognize him at first when they caught his broad smile. But then they saw the mole on his upper lip, the mole with a strand of hair, and they recognized him, and bowed hurriedly, and clothed their right fists in their left palms, and mumbled, *"gong ci far chai,"* and disappeared like a puff of smoke into the school.

Mr. Fong stepped up to the principal and right away greeted him with *"gong ci far chai."* The two hardly ever had dealings with each other. The principal was an educated man, with a diploma from a university in Taiwan, ready to rattle away the eight rules of conduct, whereas Mr. Fong's schooling consisted of a few years of grade school.

Fong Mun bowed to the principal; like the other students, he could not get over the principal's rare smile, was discomfited by his friendliness and easy manner. The principal didn't give him a red envelope. But Fong Mun did not expect it, anyway: the stinginess of the principal was famous among students and matchmakers.

Mr. Fong led Fong Mun through the gate to the school grounds, stopping to greet people he knew, the senior and junior uncles, people in the community. Some of them Mr. Fong knew way back in his childhood. Some came from the southern part of China, adjacent to Indochina, to settle in Laos. They now filled the school grounds, gathered under the antler branches of the plumeria trees, around pots of large, blooming red hibiscus.

Chairs and tables of wine and candies—trays of watermelon seeds dyed red, finger-size sugared winter-melon slices, sugared lotus seeds—were set under the plumeria trees. A few balloons rose above the cluster of antler branches of the plumeria trees.

Each of the senior uncles' wives, with a new hairdo, a happy smile, rouged lips, and manicured nails, handed Fong Mun a small red envelope. Their husbands and Mr. Fong shook hands, slapped each other's back, toasted one another with wine, burst into robust laughter.

With a few red envelopes in his pockets, Fong Mun followed his father into the main hall—the classroom for six grades, where framed notebook portraits of the past presidents of the Overseas Chinese Association were on display in a row along the two facing walls. Behind the stage hung an enlarged portrait of Sun Yat-sen. Colorful streamers flowed wall-to-wall across the ceiling.

The principal stepped up to the podium, and through the microphone on the lectern, he quieted down the room with a greeting and a brief description of the program. But it developed into a speech instead: how this gathering, this joyous occasion, was a demonstration of the community's solidarity.

Fong Mun, standing next to his father with all the

uncles and aunts, eagerly waited for the grand speech to end and the raffle to begin. He fixed his eyes on the stack of prizes on the podium. He noticed a large flat box. What could it be? A burst of applause signaled the end of the speech.

The raffle began. Each time the master of ceremonies rattled out a number, Fong Mun's heart jumped. The winners, one by one, went to the podium to claim their prizes. Fong Mun watched in despair as the pile of presents dwindled. Just when he gave up hope, he heard his number—the last one. He raced to claim his prize and could hardly wait to get home and open it.

People gathered in the school grounds and chatted. On the way out the Fongs ran into some other family friends they had not seen earlier when they came in. Another round of *"gong ci"* followed.

Mr. Fong took the long route home. On the street, peddlers, bicyclists, cabmen, vegetable vendors went on with their lives as usual. No trace of festivity had visibly touched them. All the shops run by the Chinese were closed. The Vietnamese families, too, closed their doors. The sleepy ancient royal capital became sleepier, the market more than half empty.

The Fongs reached home. As Fong Mun stepped into the house, he caught the scent of roses mingled with sweet candied fruits and incense from the altar in the cool and quiet shop. He knew who had arranged the vase of roses on the table. He peered to the right: the altar and the burning joss sticks, and a full vase of tuberoses on two sides of the altar. Tuberoses and joss sticks: Ahma had arranged these.

Ahma began to set the table for lunch. Fong Mun showed her his prize, hurrying to unwrap it, unable to figure it out, the hard cube. A box of chocolate, perhaps. Ever since he claimed the prize he had tried to guess. He fingered it in his pocket, and sitting on the back of the motorcycle on the way home he still kept guessing. A box of crayons? Candies? A toy? He unwrapped the prize and it confirmed his suspicion. He had refused to make the right guess.

Ahma told him to put the soap away. She said she had just had a mild electric shock. He looked up, startled. A mild shock, she said. With no customers to harass her, she had spent the morning in bed, mumbling or repeating a chant while fingering—bead by bead—the round string of prayer beads. Her bedroom was unlit; the only source of light came from the altar, where two bright light bulbs illuminated images of Chinese deities arranged in a row. A light bulb went off. She got shocked while replacing it. A mild shock, she told her daughter-in-law, who heard her fall from the tall stool. Jolted from the solitude of her celebration, Mrs. Fong came in and found Ahma on the floor. She helped Ahma get to her feet and walked her to her bed.

His mother later told Fong Mun, "All the praying and burning the joss sticks will do no good if she's mean to people." A punishment from heaven on the first day of the New Year.

* * *

The celebration continued for nine more days. The Fongs went to the movies, which played night and day during the festive period. A folded red card, like a wedding invitation, listed the movie program for the first ten days. The Fongs visited relatives, went to the hill of the Golden Pagoda Mountain to take pictures, with the Royal Palace in the background. The red empty booth by the gate. The two rows of palm trees with a passage in the middle leading to the front steps of the palace. The three-elephant symbol of the kingdom above the door with a gilded door frame.

After ten days of celebration, Fong Mun took the money out of the stack of red envelopes given to him by the uncles and aunts. He folded each bill flat and pushed it through the dorsal fin of a plastic carp, his bank. The money dropped into the bulging fish belly.

After ten days of celebration, Ahma removed the peach branch from the studio and put it in the ditch in the washing area by the bathing stall, to keep it alive a while longer, in the bilge water. Tiny baby peaches would appear, then wither.

After ten days of celebration, the *jong* got moldy, and Ahma threw them away.

The weather turned hot in March. Every day the sun fought to get through the door and the windows into the shop, fighting to slant from the side of the large sheet of burlap that guarded the shop against it, fighting to reach the showcase, to bleach the photos and cameras on display. In mid-afternoon the sun had moved low enough to shine past the burlap.

Under this relentless pressure, the once rosy cheeks and smiles of the faces in the photos lost their luster. But through the years the photos remained on display. Even after the color had faded. Even after the rouged smiles of the beauties had become purplish blue. Even after the soldiers had died from land-mine explosions or rifle shots.

As they cleared the table, Raymond asked, "Did you write all of the recipes from memory?"

They had put the leftovers in the refrigerator and the dishes in the dishwasher.

"All of them, yes," Fong Mun answered.

"Surely not all appeal to the American taste?" Raymond raised his eyebrows slightly.

"Only some of the dishes appear on the catering menu," Fong Mun said. "I included the others in the cookbook."

They sat down at the table. Fong Mun poured peppermint tea for them both. "My recipes represent a way of life that has disappeared. Consider the process of making *jong*. People made this particular kind only for New Year. The New Year celebration in 1973 turned out to be the last one—by 1974 the situation in Indochina had grown to a crisis." He handed a cup to Raymond. "Luang Prabang became practically deserted after the emancipation. People fled to Thailand, to France and Canada, to Australia, anywhere they could go. The Hmongs resettled as far away as in Argentina, and there are many in Europe and this country. Their children will become citizens of different countries, adopt different customs, speak different tongues. Strangers to each other." Fong Mun paused to look into Raymond's eyes.

Would Fong Mun and Raymond—who were now citizens of the same country, spoke the same language, lived in the Bay Area, and sat next to each other—despite these factors that brought them together, be strangers to each other, so that happiness and sorrow were once again hopelessly entangled? Or would Fong Mun control the timing, determine the proportion of these two malleable ingredients?

A few years ago, on his way to scout a garden in Sonoma County, Fong Mun had stopped by a fair at the Marin County Fairgrounds, north of Golden Gate Bridge. He happened on a booth where a Hmong woman had put up her embroidery for sale. She showed him her handiwork, in which she had stitched her memory of life in Laos. A simple domestic scene of a hen with her chicks gathered under her wings, under a cluster of banana trees. A scene in which a group of men on the shore (Fong Mun recognized the Brothers' jungle-green military uniforms) aimed their rifles at a group of women (Fong Mun recognized the Hmongs' outfits too) swimming across a river toward the opposite bank. Fong Mun was perhaps the only customer that day who could identify the river as the

Mekong, the men as the Brothers shooting from the Laotian shore, and the women as the Hmongs fleeing across the border. Did the fleeing come first? Were the women spotted and thus were shot at? Or did the Brothers shoot first, causing the women to flee? The embroidery left unsaid what awaited the Hmong women on the opposite shore: Thailand, freedom, or the unknown? It also left unsaid what they left behind: dead husbands, broken families? The woman and Fong Mun first spoke in English, and he told her he came from Laos, too. Had she lived in Luang Prabang? When they switched to Lao, she said she had a son like him. The way she put it made him think that her son was dead and that she spoke of him from memory. But as she rambled on, it became clear that her son was alive and well, a robust young man who majored in computer science at a state university. The woman gave Fong Mun her business card. She lived in Lake Merced.

Fong Mun sipped his tea. "Some things I had to leave out of the cookbook. Besides the question of taste, there is the problem of availability of ingredients. Even if people want to try making the capon-fat rice, where do they get a capon? And all that fat, so unhealthful.

"But my family used to make this dish for New Year, and even if I've never done it, I believe I would know how. First, extract the capon fat by frying it, the way my grandmother fried pork fat for lard. When the rice is about cooked, mix the capon oil in it. Throw some fried garlic shreds on top. Cook the rice and it'll be full of appetizing fragrance."

Raymond sipped some tea. "You didn't put it in the cookbook."

"It has lost its appeal in this health-conscious age. I've forgotten a number of New Year dishes—and I was too young to care about how they were made. The stewed duck with gingko nuts. I'll never taste it again."

"So where your memory fails, your imagination can't even make up for it?"

"How do I duplicate the dish? Through fantasy?" Dare he take such poetic license? A food reviewer had accused him of making up his recipes, of blurring the boundary between a cookbook and a novel, of allowing fiction to interfere and complicate the direct relationship between the recipe and the resulting dish. What the review implied was unsettling: that he had taken his readers in, on purpose. His unknowing readers, new to Southeast Asian cookery, ought to file a consumer complaint, alert the media to the existence of a con-artist cookbook writer, get him to confess to faking recipes to an undercover camera.

Fong Mun rubbed his cup with both hands and leaned back in the chair. "I can still catch the fragrance, but I can't picture the dish. I don't know how to conjure up the method."

"Luckily you still remember how Ahma made *jong*," Raymond said.

"Yes. But some New Year dishes are beyond retrieval." Fong Mun sighed. "And others, too, such as the coconut pudding. When I flew to the capital for summer vacation, I always went to the movie district for a bowl of this pudding."

"Why in the capital?"

"It was not sold anywhere else."

"You know how to make it?"

"No way."

"Not even through experimentation?"

Fong Mun shook his head. "I'll not taste it again in my life."

"Do you remember the color, the texture, the shape?"

After these questions, it would be selfish indeed of Fong Mun to withhold any recipes in the future. But now he was too wrapped up in the memory of a cup of refrigerated coconut pudding to think about impressing a man. "It's bowl-shaped, smooth and white, served cold with fruit cocktail. It looks like almond algar, but it's a hundred times better than the almond algar sold in dim sum places."

June 1973, Vientiane, Laos

After school ended Fong Mun's parents took him to the capital for summer vacation. They would stay with Mr. Hahn, the tailor—Mr. Fong's friend. They didn't inform the Hahns of their arrival date, dispatched no telegram or letter—and there was no telephone. They simply decided on a date, bought the plane tickets, and on that day drove to the airport, and if it was not so rainy that the flight had to be canceled, the plane would arrive on time. And the Fongs hopped on the flying engine and arrived in the capital an hour later. From the airport they took a taxi into the city.

In the alley where the Hahns lived, the Fongs got out of the taxi, unloaded the suitcases by the dusty roadside, and, carrying the suitcases and bags with sweaty palms, showed up at the Hahns' door.

Mr. Hahn was bent over, measuring a piece of fabric with a big ruler and marking it with a stumpy red pencil. When human shadows were cast on the piece of fabric in front of him, he turned, and upon the sight of the Fongs at the door, a smile spread over his thick lips.

Later in the afternoon, after the Fongs had taken a nap, Mr. Hahn showed them his factory in the back of his house. A year ago, he had boasted about owning and operating the first record-manufacturing facility in the nation. He opened the padlocked door and led the Fongs in. In the dark, stuffy hallway of the factory, stacks of records piled along the wall almost touched the ceiling, summing up the glory of the Chinese Malaysian singer on their jackets.

After producing three unsuccessful albums, Mr. Hahn modified his musical ambitions and converted the factory to a peanut oil manufacturing plant, which his investor—this very Mr. Fong—agreed was more practical. "And surely lucrative," the confident dreamer assured his skeptical investor. Failed dreams aged the partners, but new dreams kept them young, in the land of penury. In the 1950s, new to Laos, the two friends combined their resources to buy the Green Fishtail, and when Mr. Fong decided to set out for Luang Prabang with his mother in the American car, Mr. Hahn opted to stay in the capital, chose the trade of tailoring, and started a family.

To make room for Mr. Hahn's new enterprise, dusty records were shipped out, given away for charity. A set of machinery arrived and was shipped in. But even charity had no use for the records without the accompanying donation of record players; so most of the records were returned and shipped back in, now stacked in the hallway as a reminder of a grand, now soured dream.

Again Mr. Hahn boasted about owning and operating the only peanut oil plant in the nation. "But it had not been in operation for months," friends had told him. Other than a musty odor, a mixture of machine oil and the dry residue of crushed raw peanuts, no evidence of peanut oil could be found, as the Fongs toured the plant.

"Only one production so far." Mr. Fong made the remark as he surveyed the row of machines.

"The second one will begin as soon as the next shipment of peanuts arrives," Mr. Hahn hastened to explain, but didn't specify when.

When they returned to the house, Mrs. Hahn had set up the dinner table. She told Fong Mun to sit down with her children as she ladled bowls of rice. She asked Mrs. Fong to sit down too, refusing all overtures of help.

The Hahns and the Fongs chatted as they dined. They couldn't have been closer if they had been all one family. Overwhelmed by Mrs. Hahn's hospitality, Fong Mun couldn't think of anyone who could outdo her in kindness.

One afternoon, Mrs. Fong went to visit a friend and left Fong Mun under his father's care. Upstairs, the heat made Fong Mun drowsy. He heard his father's voice from downstairs. Mr. Fong kept asking Mr. Hahn when the next production would begin and Uncle Hahn said soon, after the peanut shipment arrived. But when? Again Uncle Hahn sounded vague. Comforted by his father's voice and its proximity, Fong Mun slowly closed his eyes.

Meanwhile dusk rose over the porch, wafted through the door, billowed across the ceiling above the bed, and transformed itself into a gecko. It looked about to fall off and drop on the bedside where Fong Mun dozed. He had the sensation of being stared at; he opened his eyes and found the reptile on the ceiling above him. He took a dry gulp but dared not budge.

Fong Mun inwardly called to his father. His voice traveled from the door, out the porch to the road, from the road to the thoroughfare, past the morning market, over the Laotian replica of the Arc de Triomphe, toward the countryside, toward the hills, over the mountain range. Fong Mun listened but heard only the echo. With the gecko wriggling its tail above him, he stayed still and, transfixed, heard no other voices but his own wild thoughts.

Later, his father's voice came from downstairs, through the slit between the planks of the floor. At that moment the gecko disappeared in a blink.

Footfalls striding upstairs. Mr. Fong appeared on the landing, in the white shirt and pleated pants Fong Mun had seen him in earlier. Intact, civilized. Fong Mun sprang from the bed and clung to his father.

"Why so timid?" his father chided him, and dismissed his fear of being left alone in a strange setting. "Why didn't you turn on the light? Silly."

* * *

The Fongs ate out often. When Mr. Fong took his family to restaurants on Mr. Hahn's motorcycle, his son sat wide-legged in front of him on the gas tank, holding onto it, and his wife sat sideways behind him, holding onto his waist. She wore a shawl—its two ends tied into a butterfly knot under her chin—to prevent her hair from being ruffled by the wind.

They went to places where Fong Mun had never been before: they passed street corners where *sarm-laws* were parked; they passed pharmacies selling Western medicine, French bakeries, an entire street of Indian fabric shops and tailors. A man wearing a turban stood on the sidewalk outside a fabric store. The wind brushed Fong Mun's legs. It brought on a queasiness, for an invisible gecko had climbed up his ankle.

Dusk fell. It darkened the stores, the roofs of French colonial buildings, and the sidewalks. The fountain in the center of a circle where streets converged looked blurry. Electricity poles became tall hanging vines that sent out long, wiry tendrils from one joint to another. Blurry figures moved about on the sidewalks.

Just as Fong Mun caught a yellow round light staring at him, it quickly went off. And above it a red round light lit up. Mr. Fong stopped the motorcycle.

As darkness settled, lights came alive. Some rolled down in columns and then shot back up, in the shape of words—The Pearl Suite, The New Vientiane Dining Parlor, The Crown Attic—in red and green, in purple. They glowed and, shy and mischievous, changed shapes and colors. A row of blue balls rolled counterclockwise along a rectangle and reappeared as pink, again rolling counterclockwise.

Fong Mun's father brought the Honda to a halt, switched off the headlight, parked on the sidewalk. His mother untied the butterfly knot of her shawl and folded it in her purse. His parents held his hands as he walked between them.

The smell of food, the sound of the chefs' spatulas stirring their woks, the laughter and chatter of the diners, the bright chandeliers, spilled through the open windows and doors onto the sidewalk. The tiger growl of the propane burner by the brightly lit entrance of the restaurant welcomed the Fongs. And as they entered, the rich aroma from the kitchen enveloped them.

Mr. Fong ordered—among other things—fried sparrows.

Amid his parents' talk, Fong Mun heard the blast of the propane burner, and he even dared to take a look, to verify that the blue flame under the heavy-duty wok was not the fangs of the growling tiger.

The spinning ceiling fan cast a shadow that circled the Fongs' table.

The waiter brought a plate of sparrows, fried golden red, arranged in a circle. Their necks arched backward in thin long curves that their live counterparts could never rival. Their beaks opened as if in between songs. Their wings, spread in flight, were stiff.

Fong Mun started with the best part. He crunched the skull with a bite and, while munching, savored the cranium, the gray and white matter, the ruined nasal passage, the burned beak. He worked his tongue down the neck, crunchy and delicate, and finally bit the avian structure.

At the end of the meal, the waiter brought a tray of scented hand towels to the table. Fong Mun took the towel, unfolded it, and smelled it: so cool. He rubbed his hands with it.

Afterwards the Fongs rode back to the Hahns' home, left the Honda there, and walked to the movie district for dessert.

In the district neon lights blinked merrily: strings of rainbow-colored necklaces adorned the bare neck of the night. Under the neon lights, a veil of smoke hung low. It came from the roadside vendors grilling the trademark Laotian barbecued chicken and beef tendon and meatball dipped in Tabasco sauce.

On the way to the dessert parlor across from the two cinema theaters, the Fongs turned a corner and passed the Indian pushcart selling roti, the vendor in a turban frantically spinning the dough under an oil lamp.

As Fong Mun inhaled the fragrance of the roti, he caught, to his right, the sudden sight of a shirtless youth practicing martial art in the center of a Chinese medicine store. So at home with himself. The youth positioned himself with a long pole in his hands, pure concentration. An old man stood behind the counter, the fingers of his right hand skimming over an abacus.

By the door of the medicine store, facing the roti pushcart, a cooler with glasses of chrysanthemum tea disrupted foot traffic and attracted thirsty customers. Beads of water condensed over the row of glasses.

As the Fongs passed the cooler, a waft of cool air swept their backs. The dessert parlor was a few stores away, the only place that offered Fong Mun's favorite dessert, coconut pudding with fruit cocktail.

Fong Mun held his parents' hands in case he got separated from them, lost in the mass of night treaders cluttering the street.

A song blasted from a record booth next to the theater:

Send our sorrow away.
Send it to the end of the alley.
Let the sunshine filter through the chambers of our hearts.
Send our sorrow along the flowing brooks.

The title of the song was "I Am at Your Left and Right." The theme song from a tragic movie, a tear-jerker made in Taiwan. An Indian song blasted from another record booth.

The Fongs entered the dessert parlor. The rows in the glass cooler displayed bowls of colorful desserts. Those served warm were kept in individual pots. Fong Mun ordered his coconut cocktail pudding. He wouldn't want anything else. His mother ordered a steamy bowl of lotus seeds in syrup.

After dessert, back on the street, they strolled past the two movie theaters and the two adjacent record stores. Fong Mun didn't see the records produced by Uncle Hahn—those on display were imports from Taiwan. The Fongs came to a fruit stand. Slices of papayas, two feet long, formed a row like barges along the Mekong riverfront, their ripeness the fever of sunset.

The Fongs left the movie district and came to the tree-lined thoroughfare, a row of tall, thickset longan trees on each side of the street. Some trees bore handfuls of longans, sweet round dragon eyes. The leaves made wind. A few blocks away, parallel to the thoroughfare, flowed the Mekong.

The Fongs headed for the park by the river, their sandals and slippers clattering on the pavement. The span of dark around them assumed the same seamless depth as the mountains where Fong Mun groped in his dreams.

They entered the park. The swings and the slides hung empty. Fong Mun ran to a swing. "Mother, push it for me!" he cried out. His mother pushed the swing and the wind lifted him toward the treetop.

Out of the corner of his eye he caught something sleek and squirmy by the edge of the park: the Mekong River, at night, became so barely perceptible that he would have taken it for flat land. Anyone could have walked over it, over the border, and dropped into the deep, if the breeze had not ruffled the face of the river and uncovered its treacherous muteness, the river moving busily like a centipede with its hundred hairy feet. Without the embankment, it would have climbed over and flooded the capital.

Fong Mun pointed toward the few lights flickering on the other side of the river. "Mother, is that Nongkhai?"

"So you see, the capital was the entertainment center," Fong Mun told Raymond. "You could watch TV broadcast from Thailand; you could make phone calls. The morning market alone was a few times larger than the one in Luang Prabang, which I also considered a city at the time. Ever since I'd learned the word 'city' in the first grade, I had equated it with my birthplace. If Luang Prabang was not a city, the word would have no reference for me. 'Town,' 'rural,' 'backwater'— these were harder words; the characters involved more strokes, and were reserved for mature third-graders. I continued to believe in Luang Prabang as a city as I grew older. So although the environment had changed, the notion of my birthplace as a city remained unchanged."

June 1976, The Well, Laos

Shortly after the king's dethronement, Fong Mun quit school. After he quit school he had nothing to do other than working on his garden and running in and out of the kitchen. His father would order him to leave the kitchen and go to the playground. Ahma would order him to leave the playground and go to the kitchen. It was at this time that his mother began to compare his city to a well.

One day she stopped him on his way to the narrow confines of the kitchen. "Are you contented to remain a frog in a well?"

The question caught him unprepared.

"Do you want to remain a frog forever in the well?" Her eyes were as stern as the tone of her question.

He gazed at her across the walkway. Her question and her harsh tone baffled him. When she caught him off guard that way, he became speechless. Speechlessness, plus a deliberate stare, could be used to provoke. He turned that stare on his mother. What frog? What well? He refused to answer.

"The nearsighted frog in the well thinks the whole world is no larger than this." She made a circle with her right index finger. "This is all you can see."

"Luang Prabang is a city," he corrected her.

"The city where the highest building is the three-story Lao-American Language Association."

He turned red in the face, humiliated more by the diminishment of his birthplace than by his mother's comparison of him to a nearsighted frog in a still well, perched alone on a water-lily leaf, walled in. He remembered the story of a smug frog that kept inflating itself until its stomach blew up with self-inflated air. He turned and ran off.

That night, in their bedroom, Mr. Fong asked his wife why she tended to use such a harsh tone when talking to their son. She answered him with a long stare, eye-to-eye. It spoke for her until the heaving of her chest calmed down to its normal pace. She then turned away, placed the roll of yarn in her lap, and began to knit the orange sweater, knitting while saying that Uncle K. would soon leave town to join his family in Bangkok. "Loitering is not the way to pass the time. The boy needs schooling," she said to her husband as she knit.

Auntie K. and her three younger children had left a few months earlier. The oldest son, called Big Brother, had lived in Bangkok for years.

The next morning, Mr. Fong knocked on

Uncle K.'s door. A cat scurried down from the roof of the hut. Uncle K. opened the door.

Once inside, Mr. Fong said, "In this uncertain time even school is not a safe place. It has become a military camp. The boy might get drafted and sent to Russia." Mr. Fong then told Uncle K. his plan.

Merely a neighbor, not the Fongs' sworn friend, Uncle K. agreed to help. "I can take the boy with me," he said. "We can take care of him."

Mr. Fong lowered his voice. "We will come for him in a few months."

Later in the afternoon, Mrs. Fong put the question to her son as they planted a banana tree in the garden—in the plot where Auntie K. used to grow her lettuce before she abandoned it for a new life in Bangkok.

Fong Mun stopped digging. "Will it be a short stay?"

"Yes." Mrs. Fong put the young banana shoot in the hole, and together they filled it with soil.

"For how long? Half a year?" Fong Mun stared at the young banana shoot. He would not see it grow tall and leafy and bear fruits.

"Yes, about half a year."

Fong Mun eyed his mother. His parents would have to fetch him in Bangkok later—if he went there.

"Papa and Mama will let you decide this time, to stay or leave," his mother said as she cleared away some pebbles. "You still have some time to think it over."

"If I don't go . . ."

"We are not forcing you to." She probably would not finish knitting the orange sweater in time for his departure.

That night, lying in bed next to Ahma, Fong Mun envisioned Bangkok as a city with stately high-rises, a city rampant with pickpockets. A city that would expand his horizons. He had begun to feel restless, having dropped out of school, not wanting to learn Marxist thoughts and shout them out all day. No longer a city but a town, Luang Prabang was transformed into a deep, dark well for the mind. He would become a provincial, a veritable frog. Eventually he would be drafted, sent to Russia for military training, as had happened to the dentist's two sons. Birds and people alike had fled. Why shouldn't he? Now he had the chance to test his wings, to choose to be a bird rather than a frog. So how far could he go? He could treat his going to Bangkok as a vacation, a short trip—a bait to induce his father to act. For Mr. Fong was the "host" in the household: he alone made all the decisions, and as long as he stayed in Luang Prabang, all members of the family would stay, and so far he had not mentioned a word about leaving the country. Until his buddies and acquaintances had all gone, until he found no more familiar faces in Luang Prabang, Mr. Fong would probably stay put. But if he went away, Fong Mun reasoned, then his father would have no alternative but to leave—or else the family would be separated. Fong Mun decided he would take that risk.

* * *

Ahma took out a handkerchief to wipe her eyes, speechless because what she needed to say she had already said. She held Fong Mun's hands for a while longer before she let him go.

Fong Mun, straining to keep calm, turned around to look for his mother. Ever since he had decided to go to Bangkok she had instructed him about how to behave once he got there. As she packed for him by the bedside, the suitcase open on the bed, she reminded him to be wary of pickpockets, not to carry too much cash on the street, to obey Auntie and Uncle K., and to be diligent about writing letters home. And then she told him that she hadn't finished the sweater in time. She still had one sleeve to knit. She had begun knitting the sweater with a sense of foreboding, at a time when news of South Vietnam and Cambodia filled the newspaper and radio reports. She knit the sweater with a sense of mild pleasure when the Brothers stepped into the shop to have their photographs taken, but her needles clicked angrily when the Brothers invaded her home to itemize her family's assets. She knit with a sense of alarm as she watched her son leave home to attend rallies and seminars. On the day of the king's dethronement, she held up her work and was surprised to find it deformed, her mental state in plain view: one sleeve shorter than the other, the neck too tight, the chest area cramped. She unraveled the sweater and started over. This time she knit with steady purpose. It made her knit faster. But when she thought about the consequence of finishing the sweater, she slowed down, postponing its completion. Still, with the strength of a mother, she kept knitting. She would have to give the sweater to him in person, in a different country, Fong Mun thought. His mother threw a fistful of camphor into the suitcase before she closed it.

Now, seated in an armchair in her bedroom, she told Fong Mun, "Remember Mama's word."

He nodded.

She looked calm; her voice was calm.

He tried to restrain himself, too.

She got up from the chair. Together they carried the piece of luggage out of the bedroom and handed it to a workman. She accompanied Fong Mun only to the end of the walkway; then she turned around, heading for the kitchen.

According to custom, only the young see their parents off. The custom arises out of a law of nature: the old will die before the young. It is bad luck, counter nature, for the gray-haired one to see the black-haired one off.

Fong Mun watched his mother disappear into the kitchen. He wondered why she appeared so hardened, her steps so resolute. She offered him no last-minute instruction, no words of comfort, no good-bye, and shed no tears. He got into the jeep with his father, and the workman started the jeep.

Cotton-ball clouds floated over the town, over the hillside, over Fong Mun and his father in the jeep crossing the bridge across the river Khan. The jeep bumped along on the long narrow road that cut across the open grassland, toward the airport.

Fong Mun gazed out the window of the jeep. The

old bomb craters along the runway were half-filled with rain from the night before. Two water buffalo sat soaking in one bowl-shaped crater, while a few others grazed idly by the barbed-wire fence. No plane in the sky. The new national flag hung from the flagpole outside the airport.

They waited in the airport. The prospect of leaving Luang Prabang for good made it difficult for Fong Mun even to look the workman in the eye. When the plane arrived, Fong Mun said good-bye to him. He exited the waiting room with his father, and they walked toward the plane. On the runway he looked around—at the waiting room, at the airport building, at the open grassland and the distant hillside, at the winding road to the airport, which led back home. He turned around and headed for the plane.

Mr. Fong picked the front seats. Fong Mun peered out the window. The plane took off. Within minutes it flew over the hills.

Fong Mun saw a river through the window, turbid, earthly brown, the enlargement of the meandering body of a fat earthworm. He couldn't tell what river it was. Too small to be the Mekong or the river Khan. Perhaps a tributary he had not known about? Trees along the river. Huts among the trees. A papaya tree in the middle of a clearing. Fewer stilted timber huts, thicker clusters of trees. Then no huts at all.

The plane flew over a hill and Fong Mun spotted the mossy roof and unplastered walls of a temple at the hilltop: no sign of a monk or a nun, or livestock.

Fong Mun didn't see any familiar landmarks. The

plane did not fly over the town, for a glimpse of the Royal Palace and the Golden Pagoda Mountain, of the Mekong and the coiling river Khan. If the plane had flown over the town, his mother and Ahma would have spotted it from their home. They would have gathered in the courtyard waiting to see it flying over. Fong Mun pressed his face to the window.

Quickly the trees below appeared denser and smaller. Fluffy clouds began rolling in. Patches of them glided toward, over, and under the plane. Fong Mun wished he could feel as light as the clouds. He consoled himself with the thought that time would pass as fast as the clouds riffling over the plane. A better day would soon arrive.

Fong Mun leaned back. He began to mutter the name of Guan Yin, the goddess of mercy, over and over, which Ahma had taught him to do, for safety and protection.

The prayer worked. Fong Mun did not throw up and had no headache, and the plane landed safely in the capital.

The Fongs took a taxi. As usual, they had not written to Uncle Hahn. When they showed up at his door, Uncle Hahn had his usual smile for them.

Mr. Hahn had closed the factory after the second peanut oil production in 1974, before the change of government, and he quickly sold all the oil: a few tin cans. Yet in the summer of 1976, Mr. Hahn still complained about the high cost of producing peanut oil. "Laos is not ready. The country doesn't even have enough pigs to make lard with. When we can afford enough lard, then we can think about making vegetable oil." He mumbled to himself, "The tailoring business doesn't do well, either."

Mr. Fong had been hearing his brotherly friend complaining in this way for years, even before he agreed to finance the factory.

Two days later, Mr. Fong took Mr. Hahn's motorcycle and drove Fong Mun to the Chinese embassy. Fong Mun straddled the motorcycle behind his father and held onto his father's waist as they rode through the capital.

Two rows of tall leafy trees bordered the parkway; bicycles and a few motorcycles were coming and going. To the left of the parkway, duckweeds and their lavender blossoms packed a large pond. A narrow wooden bridge zigzagged across the pond to timber houses with corrugated tin roofs.

Mr. Fong knew the streets well. Fong Mun himself would be lost in this city. The strange surroundings caused the invisible gecko to materialize and wiggle its tail over him.

In the embassy—a villa surrounded by red hibiscus bushes along the walls—people waited in the lobby for their papers.

After Mr. Fong obtained Fong Mun's passport, they went to a rice-plate eatery near the restaurant where, in the summer of 1973, they used to go for fried sparrows. Once again as visitors to the capital, in the summer of 1976, they ate out at homely eateries. But then all the fancy restaurants were shut down. People had deserted their shops and fled to Thailand.

Father and son used a fork instead of chopsticks for the plate of barbecued pork over rice. Fong Mun didn't expect that the barbecued pork would taste so good with rice and just a few pieces of crunchy cucumber.

Father and son, under the spinning ceiling fan, sat facing each other. They ate without talking, as if in fear that the passport in the father's pocket could hear their plans and would report them to the Brothers.

Fong Mun already felt like a vagrant, eating out, going from place to place for the daily three meals, eating food that strangers cooked. It made him feel—even with his father around—homeless, a drifter.

Later in the evening Fong Mun went to an Indian film, dubbed into Lao, with Uncle Hahn's two daughters. They wore plain, uninspiring clothes more suitable for their parents. Trumpet pants (bell-bottoms), supposedly in vogue, were outlawed by the Brothers, who tried to subdue any appearance of glee in the populace, so as to bring calm to the capital.

Fong Mun and Uncle Hahn's two daughters stopped at the street corner where the Indian used to busily make roti. It was outside an abandoned Chinese medicine store, its door now shut and dust-laden. Fong Mun pictured the shirtless youth he once had seen holding a long pole practicing martial art in the center of the store, amid the fragrance emanating from drawers of herbs, drawers in rows along the walls. In memory, he would remain nameless, faceless, shirtless.

The dessert parlor where Fong Mun had had his favorite coconut pudding too was closed. No more clutter or bustle on the streets. So empty that the capital looked deserted.

But movies—Chinese, Indian, and Thai films, all imported from Thailand—still played to full houses. No Brothers—at least not those in uniforms—sat in the audience. The two girls and Fong Mun had to sit in the very front row, craning their necks for three hours to watch the pair of Indian lovers extend their dancing and singing on the green hills to kissing in the corridors of a majestic palace. As they sang, the lovers ran from each other's arms and then danced toward each other again.

Right after the happy ending Fong Mun and the two girls hurried back to Uncle Hahn's before the curfew.

The next day Uncle K. came over in a taxi. Fong Mun bowed and greeted Uncle K. while his father put his luggage in the trunk.

Uncle K. kept touching his own luggage, a bag by his side.

Fong Mun parted from the Hahns, got into the taxi, closed its door.

Mr. Hahn extended his hand into the window to Fong Mun. "Take care of yourself," he told Fong Mun, heartily shaking his hand. When the taxi began to move, Uncle Hahn stepped back and waved good-bye.

Fong Mun waved back.

In the airport Mr. Fong checked in and got Fong Mun's ticket. Fong Mun tied a tag around the handle of his luggage. Mr. Fong and Uncle K. stood by the luggage and commented on the weather, the arrivals, the time. Soon, looking through the floor-to-ceiling glass wall, they spotted the plane from Bangkok. It landed and slowly came to a stop.

When they heard the jumbled announcement, Uncle K. bent down to grab his luggage.

Mr. Fong handed the luggage to Fong Mun, saying, "The boarding call. Time to go in." With his mouth clamped tight, Fong Mun took the luggage and eyed his father. Uncle K. and Mr. Fong shook hands and said farewell one last time. Then Mr. Fong turned to Fong Mun, lifted his chin to signal "Go, go." Fong Mun hurried along behind Uncle K. toward the departure gate and out to the runway.

Fong Mun got on the ladder, and when he peered over his shoulder he saw, back in the airport, behind the floor-to-ceiling glass wall, a small figure in a white shirt. Black hair. Fong Mun couldn't make out the face.

The man in the white shirt behind the glass wall waved to Fong Mun.

Fong Mun waved back. Then he turned and encountered the courteous, smiling stewardess waiting for him to hand the ticket over.

Fong Mun had stepped out of the circumference of the well. It was now sealed to him.

"I have no memory of Vientiane," Raymond said.

"I've included a number of photos of Vientiane in this cookbook." Fong Mun leaned toward Raymond to turn the page.

They had moved from the table in the dining room to the sofa in the living room. They now sat side by side, the cookbook open across their laps.

"It looks so far away."

Fong Mun pointed at a black-and-white snapshot of a tree-lined thoroughfare. "Look at the row of trees and shops." He recognized the row of leafy longan trees. He pointed at another snapshot. "This area is the movie district."

"I was just a child that last summer you were there."

"Just think, we were in the same city." Fong Mun nudged Raymond with his elbow. "Maybe you lived near the movie district."

Raymond muttered, "The barbecued pork over rice. Slices of cucumber. Refrigerated chrysanthemum tea," as if in chanting he could conjure up the experiences.

"You'll find the medicine store around the corner."

Raymond faced Fong Mun. "Do your cookbook readers make these recipes? Or do they read it for pleasure, like a novel, only it makes them hungry?"

"I used to read recipes myself—although they might be completely foreign and of no relevance to my life. For one thing, the ingredients like cheese and milk were hard to get in Laos. But reading recipes at the time connected me to a different world."

Perhaps his readers, too, used his cookbook not so much to learn to make Southeast Asian food as to lead a vicarious culinary life, to fill some longing, before they woke to their world of solid sandwiches, pasta, and Chinese food. He had yet to meet someone who put his recipes to active use.

Raymond seemed like a candidate to try out the recipes so as to have a taste of a life foreign and yet intimate. Now this young man picked up where Fong Mun left off. "Your cookbook connects me to . . ."

Fong Mun gazed at Raymond. And the pause became deliberate as neither party seemed inclined to continue; instead, each filled in the blank in his own way, guessing the other's answer.

It was the younger of the two who gave in under the weight of the pause. ". . . a past I hardly know anything about."

"My concern exactly." Fong Mun sighed. "Readers may be indifferent to this cookbook because they can't relate to it. They may find its practical value limited, its relevance questionable. I want you to care, Raymond." He reached for Raymond's hand, and registered a look in the young man's eyes that said "I know." He patted Raymond's hand.

Fong Mun chattered on, to appear unaware of Raymond's unease, also to make him more at ease. "Recipes can connect readers to a new world of gustatory promise. My mother used to read to me American recipes in the magazines she subscribed to, recipes such as how to make beef steak and apple pie—written in Chinese. According to a saying, one fills the hunger by drawing a cake. Sublimation. Reading recipes became the closest we could get to eating the food."

Raymond lifted his eyebrows. "Like watching a TV commercial?"

"Not quite. When I stayed in Bangkok, watching the hot-chocolate commercial on TV made me crave a cup of hot chocolate for breakfast. The children in the commercial looked so healthy—bright eyes and toothy grins. For breakfast we usually had plain porridge, rice boiled in water, with pickles. I never had milk, not even condensed milk. I had to imagine the taste of the rich, sweet cocoa. Reading recipes, looking at the commercials, passing by food stands and looking at the actual food itself and smelling it—it created such temptation."

"It makes you hungry," Raymond said.

"It intensifies my hunger."

1976, Bangkok, Thailand

"You're Thai," Auntie K. told Fong Mun.

They gathered inside the living room. Fong Mun sat on the floor, the only cool spot. On the sofa Auntie K. pondered whether he should have a Thai name.

"Ma, he doesn't even speak Thai," her daughter Junda reminded her.

"But since he'll stay here with us—"

"How can he have a Thai name and not speak Thai?" Junda asked.

"No hurry. We can see how things go," said Big Brother, the oldest son. At twenty-five, he was dark-skinned, heavyset, with the beginning of a pot belly.

"Not wise," Auntie K. said. "He should have a name."

The family began to think.

"Tell people you come from Taiwan," Uncle K. instructed Fong Mun.

"Taiwan?" Auntie K. looked sideways at her husband. "People will tell he's from Laos right away. Taiwan!" She said the last word with a sneer and looked away from him.

"Say it—try some words," Big Brother prodded.

Fong Mun scanned the room, then fixed his eyes on the floor, mumbled something incoherent.

The K.'s eyed one another.

"Won't pass." Junda shook her head. "You better not talk to anyone."

"Sure he can talk to people," Auntie K. said.

"Ma, his Thai is practically Lao, not Thai at all. He really shouldn't say anything to anyone." Junda turned to Fong Mun. "You'll get us in trouble."

"You can talk to people"—Auntie K. turned to him—"but choose your words carefully."

Fong Mun looked at her, becoming increasingly scared.

"Act like you're not a stranger here," she added.

"In that case, if neighbors ask we'll tell them you had gone to live in Taiwan many years ago, and now you've just come back," Junda said. "Tell them your father works in Taiwan. But you're Thai. Remember it at all times."

"If worst comes to worst, tell people you come from Esarn."

"Now that surely will give it away, Mother," Junda said. "Look at him. Who has such fair skin in Esarn?"

"He can go out in the sun," Big Brother said.

"Actually, he looks very much like a Vietnamese,"

Junda said. "Do you know," she bore down on Fong Mun, "you are an easy target, bound to get caught?"

"Once he goes out in the sun, he'll turn dark. Right, Somkit?" Big Brother winked at him with a smile.

"Somkit?" Auntie K. looked puzzled.

"Yes, Ma," Big Brother said. "What do you think of this name for him?"

"Somkit . . ." Auntie K. muttered.

"Not bad." Junda turned to Fong Mun. "From now on we'll call you Somkit."

Somkit. The name made him think of the Sunkist commercial he had seen on television: a few Thai youngsters, with their biggest grins, thrust the Sunkist bottles to the foreground while a chorus blared, "Sunkist, Sunkist, try the thirst-quenching Sunkist." He might as well call himself Pepsi.

Auntie K. always maintained that Big Brother and Junda were legitimately Thai. She claimed that she had proof: the kindergarten in Chiang Mei, a province touching the Lao border, had the record of their registration twenty years ago. "Who says we aren't Thai?" Auntie K. asked, justified.

As far as Fong Mun knew, the children were all born in Laos like him and had lived in a hut with three cats, by the pond next to his family. It had never occurred to him that Auntie K. used to live anywhere else. Not to mention that Junda was not even twenty.

On another occasion Auntie K. admitted to still learning to speak Thai. Her daughter had told her, "Ma, after six months in Bangkok, your spoken Thai still has a very strong accent. It leaks out. Just don't let anyone catch you." Alarmed, Auntie K. tried to appear calm; after all, was not Lao spoken in the northeast of Thailand, the part called Esarn? Where she used to live, she informed her neighbors.

"Lao is spoken all over Thailand except in Bangkok," she had told Fong Mun—a statement that Thai nationals would find more alarming than exaggerated, and would rush to refute, because it was the time when Thai nationalism was at its height, Thailand being surrounded by three Indochinese countries that had recently become Communist. But Fong Mun took the statement literally.

"Don't ever let anyone hear you speak a foreign language, Somkit," warned Junda.

The K.'s concluded the briefing and got ready for bed. Auntie K. splashed some rose water from a tiny bottle on her arms and face, to prevent rashes. She went to sleep with her face and arms covered with a dried layer of cool white rose water. Junda got the mat out, and the comforter, and the pillows. She and her mother slept in the living room area—blocked off by two closets that divided it into the living room on the outside and the bedroom for Uncle K. and his sons on the inside, with two sets of bunk beds.

Somkit climbed up the bunk-bed ladder to get to the big mattress on top of a wooden board mounted across the top of the two sets of bunk beds. As he climbed to the top, he saw Auntie K.'s youngest son, Ah-Dhi, already asleep in the mattress, sprawled in the middle with legs wide apart. Somkit crawled to his place on the left and cautiously moved a sprawling leg to one side. The leg felt heavy, and as Somkit lifted it, Ah-Dhi rolled over. The space was cleared. Somkit lay down.

In the living room Junda told her mother she wanted to make *phat-Thai* for lunch the next day.

A few moments later the bunk-bed ladder creaked: Big Brother climbing up. He had just finished washing himself. Somkit closed his eyes, knowing that Big Brother had only his underwear on. Big Brother climbed to the far right.

As the first step to acquaint Somkit with life in Bangkok, Junda took him to the market. "So you'll know how to go there next time," she said, "in case I need you to get groceries." She went to the market twice a day, once in the late morning to shop for lunch and once in the late afternoon for dinner.

They didn't have far to go: part of the market was downstairs, below the apartment building. As they plodded down from the fourth floor to the first, they heard the music from the jukebox below.

Somkit had never heard it before. Junda told him, "Here people listen to music in English." In the following weeks he would hear the rock-and-roll over and over as he passed the jukebox. So melodious.

A few Thai men, in shorts and with the top of their shirts unbuttoned, sat idly at a table across from the jukebox drinking Coca-Cola. Junda and Somkit passed them and, along the way, the *phat-Thai* stand, the oyster crepe stand, and flower stands selling lotus and wreaths of orchids.

They stepped up the sidewalk to the street. Cars coming and going. Honks were volleyed between motorcycles and taxis. Labyrinthine traffic created a murky screen of exhaust.

Junda grabbed Somkit's hand. "Use care when crossing the street," she instructed, in Lao, after she'd made sure no one could overhear her. "This neighborhood is called Din Dang. And this, the *tuk-tuk*." She pointed at a three-wheel motorcycle cab passing them. They waited for the traffic to slow down. "We can cross later," Junda said, letting go of Somkit's hand.

They plodded along the stretch of the market outside the row of uniform four-story flats. At one stand, she showed him how to identify the variety of spices: the green paste, the red paste, the red one mixed with curry, or the yellow one with ground ginger. She showed him the round green and purple pea look-alikes: they had stems, not peapods. "They taste as bitter as Chinese medicine," she told him.

They smelled something good and followed the aroma to a stand nearby. A woman was frying something in a big wok of bubbling oil. "Fried fish cake," Junda said, pointing at the mound of reddish-brown disks on a large round tray. She bought half a baht's worth. She offered him the fish cakes in the banana-leaf cone.

He took a piece, munched. "What's in it?"

"String beans." Junda then said, *"Aroy mark ca!"*

Aroy mark meant very delicious, he knew. But he

hesitated, afraid of liking the mouth-watering fish cake too much because then he would begin to crave it. It took money to buy something one liked to eat or have. He would keep thinking about the flavor of the fish cake and worry about what would happen to him when his money ran out. He would not have any peace. Better not to have too much craving for delicious or beautiful things, such as potted plants, colorful Thai desserts, a magazine, going to movies, things that gave pleasure. Better not want.

He tried two pieces of fried fish cake and let Junda have the rest. She could afford to enjoy it.

The stands open for business were scattered here and there with a small selection of produce. Most of the stands were covered with a tarp. "See the market. It's thirty flats long."

Somkit didn't know that Junda exaggerated, until he discovered by himself that the market covered merely a certain stretch along the row of flats, and only on weekends did the vendors stretch the boundary and set up their stands on the sidewalk, too.

"I usually don't shop in this section," Junda went on. "I go to the other side."

Time to cross the street. They braced themselves. She said, "Can't act mousy." She held his hand, took a deep breath, looked left and right, and dashed. Somkit dashed along. They got ahead of the car coming from the left and stopped in the middle of the street, on the divider; and seeing that buses, *tuk-tuk*s, and trucks coming from the right were still a distance away, they ran.

Junda said, once they reached the sidewalk, "Unlike in Laos, you can't just stand and wait for the street to clear."

Somkit nodded.

"Wait till you see the traffic at Pratunam and Yaowarad."

They went into a dark passage, through a large multistory building under construction—more flats. The passage led to a market, cool and shady, wet and dirty, enclosed by three-story buildings which blocked out the sun most of the time. Somkit had to hold his pajama pants above his ankles so they would not soak in puddles of dirty water. Junda sauntered ahead because she wore a skirt.

"I'll teach you how to bargain," she turned to Somkit. "Watch me." She walked up to a butcher, who used a fan, the shape of a bodhi leaf, to chase away the flies mobbing the meat stand.

The butcher had a round belly like that of the Buddha ThusCome and smiled also like ThusCome. The smile of eternal bliss. The butcher took a look at Junda: her almond eyes and cherry mouth, her shiny hair which grew down past her waist and glistened. He could tell she was Chinese. She was younger than she appeared. Her spoken Thai sounded crude and affected. He spoke to her in Taeju, a dialect widely spoken by the Chinese in Bangkok.

Somkit couldn't understand Taeju. He stepped back, watching Junda bargain.

She pointed to a piece of lean meat and spoke in her home dialect to the butcher. They gestured back and forth. Then the eternally smiling Buddha picked up a shiny knife and slit a piece of meat. He put it on a kilo scale and pointed to it and turned to eye Junda. They talked some more. He took the meat from the scale and cut off one more slice.

While Somkit stood by, a nearby merchant's radio played a lyrical Thai song. It stirred him. If he had understood the lyric—it was a patriotic song—he would have been moved to pick up a rifle to defend Thailand against the potential threat from its Communist neighbors. In the following months he would hum the tune as a result of repeatedly hearing the song on the radio.

Junda bought the rest of the ingredients needed for *phat-Thai:* dry salted shrimp (the tiny pink kind), dry rice noodles, bean sprouts, chives, dry tofu, eggs, some dry, diced icicle radish.

Junda and Somkit came up the stairs to the fourth floor. As they approached the unit, Auntie K., dressed in a deep yellow blouse and a pair of dark pants, shiny shoes, her gray hair newly dyed black, was about to close the door and leave. She asked Junda if she had all the ingredients for *phat-Thai.*

Junda said yes.

"Do you remember the steps?" her mother asked.

"I remember."

"Don't get them mixed up."

Auntie told Somkit to have lunch with her kids, because she was going to Yaowarad, the Bangkok Chinatown.

* * *

Junda's two younger brothers helped her cook because she had decreed, "Your hands can't remain idle if you want to eat."

Somkit had winced, just as if she aimed the words at him. He bit his lower lip and started to help.

"You can wash the chives. Do you know how to cut them finger-length?" Junda pointed.

Somkit had seen his grandmother cut green onions, and the chives looked like green onions. "I know how," he answered.

On the rear balcony, converted to a cooking area, Junda diced the piece of dry tofu, soaked the bundle of dry rice noodles. After it softened, she put it in a colander. She heated up the wok over the propane-burner stove, added just enough oil to the wok. She then threw in the rice noodles, stirred them with a spatula, added the chives, the diced tofu cubes, a pinch of dry shrimp and dry icicle radish, a pinch of ground peanuts.

While Junda stirred the mixture, her two brothers added some more oil to it and threw in bean sprouts, and Somkit shook in some fish sauce from the bottle, according to her directions.

"I didn't expect the noodles would get so dry." She stirred the mixture. "Lower the fire," she told her youngest brother, Ah-Dhi.

He twisted the knob—too briskly—and turned off the fire.

She screamed, "You moron! Can't you do a thing right?"

The boys scrambled for the matchbox. Ah-Dhi

looked at Junda and, hesitantly, handed the box of matches to her. It was wet.

"Who did it? Who?" Junda yelled.

Her second-youngest brother flinched. She stared down at him hard. His mouth trembled and his voice came out shaky: as he hurried through washing the bean sprouts, he had spilled the water.

Junda whirled around to twist his ear, sending him into instant howling. When she let go, his ear and face had become pig-liver red. He dropped on the floor, twisting his waist and thrashing his feet, howling to heaven and earth. She twisted his other ear, yelling, "I'll twist some more if you don't stop."

She turned to Ah-Dhi. "Why are you standing there? Go get the matches."

"I don't have the money," he said, faltering.

She threw her hands in the air. "Good. So none of you will eat. None of you!" She bolted inside.

The boy on the floor kept on whimpering.

Somkit stood against the wall, watching him.

Ten minutes later Junda appeared at the kitchen door. She threw the coin on the floor. The coin rolled to a corner and lay flat. "Get the matches."

Ah-Dhi picked up the coin and hurried off.

Junda turned to her second-youngest brother, on the floor. "Still crying? Stop this second!"

"I'll tell Mother," he whimpered.

"So now you threaten me, huh?" She made out to slap him. But even before she reached him, he started to howl, just as if she already had hit him. "Stop!" she yelled.

The wok had cooled down.

The displays of temper, all of it, subsided half an hour later. Lunch began peacefully.

"It has a different taste," Junda mumbled as she tasted the messy but colorful *phat-Thai*. "I put the same ingredients as what they sell downstairs. Same ingredients. What could have gone wrong?"

After lunch Junda hurried her brothers to clean up. Ah-Dhi, wiping the table, swept scraps of food onto the floor. Dishes cluttered the wash basin. Junda kept chastising her two younger brothers for eating so much. She complained and worried about Big Brother losing his lob.

Somkit remembered his position. He had no intention of proving what Junda had accused her younger brothers of being, a sluggard waiting to be fed. He would have to earn his lunch. He turned on the tap, filled the wash basin, fetched the detergent, grabbed a sponge. He crouched down, like his servant in Laos used to do, and began to wash the dishes.

Early in the evening Junda's friend came over. Phrases of Lao slipped from the Mandarin he and Junda spoke in. So Somkit knew the visitor came from Laos too, an unwelcome guest in Bangkok, a fugitive just like him.

Big Brother had just returned from work and had taken off all his clothes except his underwear to cool off. He wrapped a towel around his waist, came to the living room, and sat with the visitor on the sofa while Somkit and Junda, her legs folded sideways, sat on the floor.

The visitor jested about Big Brother's garb. He asked Big Brother why not just wear the underwear, why bother with the towel? Junda and Big Brother chuckled.

The visitor addressed Big Brother. "I know where to get some sexy underwear. It'll look very nice on you."

Again Big Brother chuckled, revealing his dimples. "In what way?"

"Very flimsy," the visitor said, rubbing his fingers to show the feel of the fabric.

Junda doubled up with laughter, and amusement animated Somkit's eyes.

"Very thin, the cloth, unlike the regular kind of underwear," the visitor continued. "It's very comfortable, barely there. Now, since you like to get comfortable at home, wouldn't you like to try a pair?" They all laughed. "Why not?" the visitor probed. "They're very easy to get."

"How do you know the details of the underwear so well?" Big Brother asked. "Have you tried it? Do you have a pair on now?"

It was the visitor's turn to blush. Junda shook all over with laughter.

"Are you wearing a pair?" Big Brother prodded on. "Show us yours. They must be very comfortable."

"Look at you, blushing all over!" Junda pointed at her friend—accepted by her family as her boyfriend. He blushed even more, smiling with sheepishness.

Big Brother said, "I go for the comfort. You know,

this unit on the top of the building gets so hot in late afternoon. To be sexy is not the point."

Laughing, the visitor reassured Big Brother, "Really, no need to explain. I know. I know."

Big Brother kept chortling, unaware that their jokes, in a foreign language, had leaked through the jalousies.

After their laughter subsided, Big Brother then mentioned, "My sister told me you plan to enter the refugee camp. When will it be?"

"Soon."

The remainder of a smile disappeared from Junda. She gazed down at the floor.

Somkit and the two kids watched TV on the floor while on the sofa Auntie K. asked her daughter, "Are you following him?" She cautioned, "Don't trust men. He shouldn't be your reason for going abroad, for adopting a different tongue and a new citizenship, for leaving home to be thousands of miles away, making a foreign country your new home. Think twice. Learn from my lesson."

"I can take care of myself in the refugee camp, Mother."

"I know you can. I know you have sense. Of all my children you and your big brother are the two with sense."

Junda gave her reasons, "Once in France, I'll get a job and send you money. I can lighten Big Brother's burden."

Auntie K. nodded. "Your brother is the only rice-bowl earner in this family so far. There could have been one more." She snorted.

"Mother—"

"I don't care if your father hears me. He needs to work! This is Bangkok, not Laos. Life is different here." Then Auntie K. sighed. "I know it'll take some time for your big brother's career to take off. Going to France might be a solution."

"One day he will make it," Junda said. "He'll succeed. One day you won't have to worry about rent and the three daily meals anymore." She turned to her younger brothers watching TV.

A cup of rich, steamy chocolate with condensed milk, the Jasmine brand, posed in the foreground. Somkit could smell it already as he watched the commercial. He swallowed an empty mouthful.

"Just keep stuffing that useless mouth and nothing else, the two of you. Eat up the money and we'll be out on the street," Junda chastised her brothers.

Somkit stiffened. He tried to rationalize: Junda was scolding her brothers, not him. But he represented an extra mouth to feed. He couldn't deny the fact.

A lump clogged his chest. Daily he offered to go to the market, mop the living room floor, help around the kitchen, wash dishes. He tried not to be an idle mouth fed for free.

"Now I see the kitchen too is as much a teenager's territory as the playground." Fong Mun gazed out the window to the bay.

Late afternoon, still overcast. Murky rain clouds pressed low.

"So you learned to cook by helping Junda in the kitchen," Raymond said.

" 'You all must help if you want to eat,' she ordered. I stayed by her side, handing her fish sauce if she needed it, and washing dishes. In this way I learned a number of Thai dishes from her, and I've put them in the cookbook. Some kids find the playground as unfamiliar as others find the kitchen."

"Now you've turned the kitchen into a play-ground."

"Yes. An adult playground." Fong Mun gazed at Raymond and decided to risk it and tell more. "But even at that time, in Bangkok, the kitchen—not even a real kitchen at all but the back porch of a cheap housing unit—provided more safety than the outside world."

A few days after the talk with her mother, Junda greased her long hair with olive oil, her own beauty formula. She changed her clothes, wore a dress that made her look like a lady with book learning, and sat in front of the compact mirror holding a lipstick. As she gazed into the mirror and applied the lipstick, she asked Somkit if he wanted to go with her to look for a job. She could show him other parts of Bangkok.

They tried a few boutiques in Siam Square, went to a nightclub, met the manager there. As a last resort, they entered a newly built shopping area near Siam Square. Most of the structure remained unpainted. Only a few stores were open. Junda took Somkit to a cosmetic shop. She started talking to the Indian woman there—an Indian Thai, dressed in a sari.

The Indian woman took out a lipstick from the showcase and asked Junda to demonstrate its use. Junda moved to the mirror. The woman stood behind

Junda and watched her use the lipstick. The woman nodded, said she liked Junda's work. "But the shop is not busy enough yet. I opened it just recently. The business will depend on the guardian of the shop."

She showed the two visitors the finger-size glass case above the door, on the lintel. "Not only will he bring business, he'll also watch the store for me after I go home at the end of the day. He comes out from that case at night to guard the store. I hear movements—a boy's laughter."

Somkit had learned about the boy spirit, revered in Thailand, from the soap opera based on the boy spirit's life. Auntie K. had told Somkit about the early episodes. "He was killed long before your arrival, his body soaked in a special liquid, to shrink him small enough to fit in the glass case."

Big Brother, too, had once attended a ceremony in which a master monk invited the boy spirit to manifest himself. "We couldn't see him," Big Brother had told his family, "but clearly he was present. He laughed and jumped around the room, playing with the furniture. We heard footfalls on the walls and the ceiling. The monk asked him some questions, and he chuckled a lot when he answered. He wanted to play, just like a child."

The saleswoman pointed at Somkit and asked Junda, "Your sister?"

He blushed.

Junda turned around. She laughed. "No, he's a boy."

"Is he?" The woman pressed her hand on her forehead. "All the time I thought he's a—"

"It's his hair," Junda said.

Somkit's hair had grown long enough to cover his ears.

"Just like a girl."

Somkit wished he had the supernatural power of the boy spirit, so no one could embarrass him and tease him in public for appearing girlish. A sissy! Although the salesperson didn't say it outright, that he was a *katoy*, he knew he was an effeminate boy. But to be pointed out as a girl still disturbed him. Such attention made him jumpy. But this he could endure. He feared more the discovery of his illegal status. He couldn't risk going to a barber and be caught unable to speak Thai. Long hair? He admitted he liked it. It suited him better than a crew cut. Girlish? So be it. He would rather pass for a girl than get caught as an alien with an expired visa. Still, an immunity to taunts would make life easier. The supernatural power would also enable him to buy all the food without any worry about using up his allowance, which his parents had entrusted to the K.'s. Better yet, he simply needed to use the power to absorb the drink, free of charge, when the hot cocoa commercial appeared on TV. He could conjure the cocoa right out of the TV set and instantly gratify all his craving.

He could use the power to shut out Junda's complaints.

With no job, Junda started to pack.

One early morning, before the capital woke up,

Big Brother took Junda in a *tuk-tuk* to the central train station. The underwear expert joined them there. Big Brother bought the ticket, handed Junda her luggage, and saw her board the train with her boyfriend to Nongkhai, a northern province, where the refugee camp was.

"My Thai has not improved," Fong Mun wrote in a letter to home. "When I hear a Thai speak, I still don't have a clue." He remembered Junda's words: "It shocks me you still can't make out what people say. After four months already. It's so basic, almost like Lao."

Weeks later, he found a letter under the door— from Laos. He checked the back of the letter. It looked sealed, no trace of a tear. He took the letter to read by the stairs.

His mother wrote that slowly, through time, he would learn Thai. Be patient—she ended with this advice. No mention of when the family would leave Laos.

A neighbor came to the hallway to water her potted plants by the side of the balcony. A few doors down the hall, Somkit sat by the stairs, not to cool off but to brood. He didn't notice her. He sat still, eyebrows tangled in gloom. When she first saw him there, she had meant to go over and talk to him, to ask him why he sat there so quietly, to suggest he play with her son. She had often seen Somkit leaning on the handrail, gazing at the lush tropical plants she grew in her section of the front balcony, which she had converted to a garden. But when he saw her he looked so frightened (would she find out he was from Laos and hiding illegally in Bangkok?) and hostile (did she see him as a girl?), ready to wince (at the pointing finger), to flee (else his spoken Thai would betray him), she suppressed her intention of walking up to him. She went about watering her plants instead, ignoring him.

Shortly after she had gone indoors some children came to the hallway to jump rope. The rope in their hands was made with rubber bands strung together. It didn't occur to them to question Somkit's presence. He watched them skip rope. If he talked to them, they probably couldn't tell if he spoke real Thai, or Lao, or Lao Esarn. Maybe they would mention to their parents the oddness of his speech: a knowing ear would pick up the Lao in it, a loud mouth would report him to the police.

One of the children's older sisters showed up with a few of her friends, all boys. They brought along a tape recorder, to practice their hip-bumping dance. Somkit watched the girl turn with the song and bump her partner's readily turning hip. Both of them turned the other way to bump hips again, while their hands painted the air with broad strokes, showing how a river would bend, how a ribbon would wave, how a hand would catch it. They hadn't a care.

The other boys gathered around the dancing couple and softly tapped their feet with the music, waiting for their turn.

The stranger from Laos kept away from them. Never spoke. So to them he appeared unfriendly—the question of his nationality or foreign, illegal status didn't occur to them. They simply ignored him.

He watched them. The music roused him and made him feel like doing the bumping dance, just to stop brooding for a second. He itched for movement. If he danced, who would be his partner? He glanced at the boys.

He wished he could speak Thai as fluently as Auntie's sons did—but even if he could, he dared not speak to the boys. They would treat him as a *katoy*. If he wasn't a sissy, why would he want to dance with one of them and not with the girl? They would gang up on him, tease him, laugh at him.

To Auntie K. his brooding signified his homesickness. She checked herself, delayed having a serious talk with him, for fear that he would burst into tears at the mention of his parents. She went about her own business, trusting that his troubles would build his character.

Early one morning, as he sat by the stairs, he felt a change in the weather. The wind became drier and chillier. When it got windier, he rose to leave and saw a middle-aged man coming up the stairs with a bag under his arm, as if looking for shelter.

The man broke into a grin and stopped.

"Uncle Hahn?" Fong Mun called out in Cantonese. "Is it Uncle Hahn?"

Uncle Hahn smiled wider, greeted Fong Mun, and

resumed coming up the stairs until he stood in front of him.

"When did Uncle Hahn get here? Where will Uncle Hahn stay? How long will Uncle Hahn stay in Bangkok?" He fired off a string of questions all in one breath while holding Uncle Hahn's hand and leading him inside the unit.

Uncle Hahn rattled at high volume in Cantonese. Fong Mun forgot that neighbors along the hallway might overhear the foreign tongue and get suspicious—they might see the stranger, report them, spy on them. Uncle Hahn's appearance would give him away too: dark, greased hair, a loose, faded white shirt, a pair of loose brown trousers. He gave every sign of being a Vietnamese living illegally in Bangkok.

Auntie K. asked Fong Mun to offer Uncle Hahn a cup of tea.

Uncle Hahn hastened to decline, purely out of social convention. As he took the cup of tea from Fong Mun's hands, he said, "Ah-Mun, you've grown taller."

"He misses home," Auntie K. told Uncle Hahn.

Fong Mun glanced at Auntie K.

"Oh? You must want to see your father," Uncle Hahn said.

Fong Mun said yes. He had been in Bangkok for six months and had not seen his family in all that time. His father had not acted.

"You're a big boy now, ought to learn to take care of yourself. Right?" Uncle Hahn smiled kindly. He said he had a letter, then took out an envelope from his shirt pocket and gave it to Fong Mun. "I know you'll want this, too." Uncle Hahn took out a sweater from the bag. "Your mama sent you this."

"She knit it, didn't she?" Auntie K. asked as Fong Mun unfolded the orange sweater.

Fong Mun nodded.

"She sends it to the boy for use during the cold season," Uncle Hahn said.

"It won't get really cold here and he probably won't need it. Better put it away in the suitcase," Auntie K. instructed Fong Mun.

She then asked Uncle Hahn how he had found the place. He said he took a taxi. Fong Mun wondered how Uncle Hahn got around without speaking Thai or Taeju.

Uncle Hahn said he planned to check out the refugee camp in Nongkhai. Again Fong Mun wondered what would Uncle Hahn do if the officials searched the bus he took. Fong Mun looked to Auntie K.

She neglected to warn Uncle Hahn about the police raid. Instead, she sighed. "If I knew we'd end up in Thailand . . ." She always told people she used to live in Bangkok twenty years ago. "Why did we leave in the first place? Why didn't we settle in Thailand? Almost twenty years in Laos, only to end up in Thailand to start over."

Uncle Hahn sighed deeply, resting his hands on his lap. "No matter where you run, you keep running. The same with me. From China to Vietnam, running from the Japanese. Then from Vietnam to Laos, running from the Communists. And now running from the Communists again. Running all my life." His voice trembled. He took out a handkerchief from his trouser pocket to wipe his eyes.

"I keep telling my children I must have done something awful in my past life, so now I'm punished for it, paying for my karma," Auntie K. said.

"We're too old to start over."

"The Thais are afraid. Where will they go? Communist neighbors on the east and north, the sea on the south."

Uncle Hahn put away his handkerchief. He told Auntie K. he would go to Nongkhai in two days. He wrote his hotel phone number on a piece of paper.

Fong Mun called him the next day. He paid ten *satungs* to use the grocer's phone. He dialed and let it ring only once, but when no one answered, he hung up. He didn't wait for it to ring too long, his first time using a phone.

Uncle Hahn had gone to Nongkhai. He returned to Bangkok a few days later and showed up in the flat. This time he seemed less like a stranger and more like a legitimate guest in Bangkok: already his presence seemed less conspicuous. He reported on his trip: the Nongkhai refugee camp was cold, a lot colder than Bangkok.

Had he seen any friends or acquaintances? Yes, lots of familiar faces. Uncle Hahn gave a few names: so-and-so had left the camp to resettle in France; so-and-so just had an emigration interview; so-and-so had recently arrived in the camp. Did he find it tolerable, the condition in the camp? Quite tolerable. Did that mean the trip had facilitated his decision making? Silence. Surely he didn't go to the refugee camp just to see friends? No, no, surely not. Did the trip then serve its purpose? Most definitely. What purpose did it serve? Uncle Hahn declined to be more explicit.

Implicitly, then: Uncle Hahn's trip was a setup. He went to scout the camp less for himself than for the person who had sent him. Yes, he was an emissary sent by none other than Mr. Fong. The trip to Thailand, the surprise visit, the casual appearance amid the paranoia of the Thais, served two purposes: first, to see how Fong Mun fared (why else would Mr. Hahn visit Fong Mun, who was no son or nephew of his?), and second, to pave the way for the Fongs' arrival in Thailand (for Mr. Hahn must have made inquiries about how to be admitted to the refugee camp).

Auntie K. had sensed a hidden meaning behind the ready smile of Mr. Hahn when she sat down with him.

Having completed his research and mission, he and Fong Mun, now Somkit, parted with the implicit, mutual assurance that they would meet again. Uncle Hahn flew back to Laos.

The streets were flooded. The *tuk-tuk* and the buses and motorcycles and taxis splashed sheets of brownish orange water. The water in the market reached the ankles, soaked the lawns below the apartment buildings where Somkit stayed. The jukebox and the coffee tables and the stands stood soaking in water. Bangkok became a city of water.

The rain let up one afternoon. Somkit listened to the radio, a program hosted by a television actress. He had followed it for months now. He had been going through the stations one day, looking for the melodious patriotic songs, when he heard a clear, calm, quiet voice, her Thai accessible, and he listened. A week later he heard that same clear, calm voice again as he searched through the stations. As before, he found the station by chance. And as before, he listened.

Every week the hostess's audience wrote to her for advice on their personal problems. Somkit listened to her summary of the letters and her suggestions, offered with simplicity and in such a reassuring, intimate tone. The half-hour program, once a week, seemed too short. From the fan mail she read, Somkit knew the hostess had appeared on television, but he didn't recall ever having seen her.

Somkit tuned in with anticipation. He had not heard from his family for months now. As he listened to the program, his mind grew calm, quiet, clear. He forgot, for the moment, his fear of getting caught, his fear of being separated forever from his family, his fear of using up his allowance, his hunger for a cup of cocoa and other food, and the problems that arose from being a boy who looked like a girl.

He soaked in the hostess's voice as if it were a soothing bath. He understood her Thai. But when she announced good-bye, he still wanted to soak in the bath. He became resentful as she pulled the stopper and her voice drained away. The surface of his mind became ruffled, roiling, heaving.

Just then Auntie K. interrupted his listening and

sent him to the market to get some fish cakes. He reluctantly turned off the radio.

As he reached the bottom of the stairs—floods everywhere—a fish swimming by the staircase was startled off. A small vortex disappeared from the face of the water. Somkit's high-heel slipper would be of little use in keeping him dry. Might as well enjoy getting wet. He stepped down the staircase into the water. Something slid past his ankle. A frog, or a snake? A few children, half-naked, played in the watery lawn.

Watching them, Somkit daydreamed about swimming in the lawn. School would start in a month, but if the rain kept on, students would have to row to school or swim down the sidewalk. Boats would replace cars. Somebody would get drowned.

Somkit sauntered along the gutter, hoping to see holes on the mud bank, the size of a coin, eel lairs. He didn't find any.

As he turned the corner and daydreamed about casting a trawl net into the watery lawn, to catch fish and shrimps, a police car drove into the flooded side street. Four policemen jumped out, splashing water as they touched ground. They lunged into Somkit's building, stomped upstairs to the fourth floor, swept past the gawking residents in the hallway, stopped outside a unit, pounded on the floor.

Auntie K. opened it.

Meanwhile, at the market, Somkit paid for the fish cakes. Some of the vendors had moved their stands onto boats, rowing them to hawk goods. He pictured some of the eels and catfish escaping from the cages and swimming freely, gliding past his feet.

He reached the apartment building, went upstairs. In the hall, Auntie rushed to him. "Put everything down. Quick. Go pack."

"Pack?"

They hurried indoors.

"We're leaving here. Go pack now. Quick. You need to get out. They'll release Big Brother. Nothing serious."

She would go to stay with a friend in another province, she said as she shoved her blouses and a sarong into a travel bag.

In fifteen minutes Somkit, carrying his clothes in a small bag, left the flat with Uncle K. and the two boys. They went in a *tuk-tuk* to the bus terminal for fear the police might search the train. Uncle K. told the boys they were going to visit a friend of his in the countryside for seven or eight days, until the whole thing blew over, but certainly the police would release Big Brother soon, just something the police needed to clear up and would do so in no time, his son was a hardworking boy, very pious, they couldn't lock him up, he was a legitimate Thai citizen, not a rebel, but until the police settled the matter, they should all stay away from Bangkok, where the pollution got so bad just breathing would make him cough, he had a friend in the countryside he had not seen in years, ever since he had made the mistake of moving to Laos, they had lost touch for twenty years, time for a visit, time for some fresh clean air in the countryside.

* * *

Around midnight the bus pulled into a stop—a structure with a corrugated tin roof—somewhere in the countryside. A few hawkers swarmed forward as soon as the bus pulled up. A kerosene lamp lighted the area. Except for the small lighted stop, seamless dark everywhere.

Most passengers managed to stay awake. The K's and Somkit feared that the police might show up at the door demanding everyone to show identification. But no police got on the bus. Instead the uproar came from the hawkers, whose hunger for selling was as intense as Somkit's hunger for what they sold.

"Barbecued chicken!" "Roast coconuts—roast coconuts!" the hawkers called out as each of them, patrolling outside the bus along the windows, raised a large, round bamboo tray above his head to give the yawning passengers a view of the food.

Somkit had had little to eat since Auntie K. rushed him to pack, get out of the apartment, and go to the depot, rushed him out of Bangkok into the middle of nowhere. The roast coconuts in a hawker's tray looked burned on the outside. He imagined the rich, sweet, buttery taste of the flesh, the result of roasting.

He had never eaten one before, but had always craved it, ever since he had seen it sold in the Thai market. He stared at the roast coconuts longingly, trying not to want one. He reminded himself to be content, telling himself to wait until the day he could afford it. His mind quieted.

The driver started the engine. The passengers

closed their eyes. The hawkers walked away from the bus and returned indoors. The bus ride continued in the dark.

After twenty years without communication, the sense of familiarity between Uncle K. and the host remained as strong as ever. When Uncle K. showed up in their tea shop with the boys, he brought more than a surprise to the host and his wife, Mrs. Impeccable.

The couple jumped from their chairs when they saw the guests enter, and Mrs. Impeccable's limbs went weak, her head light and febrile. After several quick intakes of breath, she moved forward to receive the guests with open arms and a clearer head. "Two boys and a girl!" she exclaimed.

Somkit flushed. He felt eyes riveting on him, and for a moment all was still. He felt more alarmed than embarrassed: What had he become? Half boy, half girl? Less of a boy, more of a girl? Why did people always single him out?

The hostess meant no harm. But Somkit felt wounded each time a stranger made the mistake. He tried not to betray any sign of effeminacy: he sat rigidly, walked rigidly, shut his mouth to hide his voice, fixed his eyes on the ground.

He could stay away from the kitchen. Tough it out with the boys on the basketball court, work himself into a sweat, pant like an overworked horse. Get in the sun, have dark skin. He could act rough, speak rough, and look tough. Become a hooligan. Why wouldn't he?

The truth was, he liked to look pretty: keep his eyelashes long, grow his hair thick and long, messy—he liked that look. The *wahwah* look.

He fidgeted as Uncle K. clarified the misunderstanding.

"I thought it was a girl." Mrs. Impeccable slapped her thigh, put on her antique glasses with thick opaque lenses, and, squinting hard, leaned forward to within a few inches of Somkit.

Somkit's first reaction was to lean back, away from Mrs. Impeccable's scrawny face, squinting eyes, and bristling nose. His hair again, he knew, and knowing too that by blushing he appeared even more girlish. His blush deepened.

As Somkit fidgeted under the microscopic examination of Mrs. Impeccable, Uncle K. explained that Somkit was not his son.

Somkit understood some spoken Taeju, and Uncle K.'s explanation made him feel even more closed off: unrelated, uninvited, illegitimate. He scanned the tea shop, glanced toward the host and his wife, Mrs. Impeccable. Somkit caught her bespectacled eyes—still scrutinizing him! Clearly his appearance amused her. His mouth clamped shut.

The host served tea and voiced his concern about the situation in Bangkok.

Uncle K. nodded, and mentioned the police raids, the number of Vietnamese Communist rebels caught hiding in all corners of the capital, the amount of leftist propaganda confiscated and burned on Sanam Luang, where Bangkok residents went kite flying on week-ends.

"Your visit is long overdue," Mrs. Impeccable remarked to Uncle K. "Good timing. You'll like the countryside. No police will bother you."

"Are we rebels? I just want my son to have a good career so he can support the family."

"The Thais are paranoid," said the hostess.

"With reason," her husband added. "The number of Vietnamese rebels caught hiding in Bangkok is alarming."

"The police will catch anyone not Thai."

Mrs. Impeccable's comment startled Somkit.

The countryside did prove to be a safer place. Maids prepared the three daily meals, washed dishes, and handwashed the clothes. The fugitives from Bangkok did not have to earn their keep by doing housework.

Even if they knew Somkit was unrelated to their old friend Uncle K., the host's family did not treat Somkit differently. Each day they served dinner at four, and after dinner they sat around and chatted. Everyone went to bed by eight. The K.'s did not feel pressured to leave, even after a stay of six weeks.

For dinner the host served a variety of dishes which Somkit had not tasted before. One dish appeared repeatedly on the dining table: glutinous rice cooked with minced dry mushroom, minced sausage, and dry shrimp.

Somkit had seen the servant mix them in as she cooked rice. How convenient, he had thought then.

Just throw everything in. Mix it with rice. Dinner in one stroke, convenient and delicious. The aroma from the dry mushroom and sausage and dry shrimp got trapped in the rice until served.

Shortly after he'd arrived, Somkit got hold of a radio from the host's servant. At four-thirty he checked the stations. He tried again for the next few days, at four-thirty, at five. He heard news, commercials, love songs—in other words, the bathwater was either too hot or too cold, not the soothing voice offering the therapy of advice. Frantic, he pictured the voice receding down the drain, being sucked further and further down the subterranean eternity.

"Isn't the country nice?" the host asked Somkit after dinner one day, in Thai.

They all sat in the kitchen, their ears beset by the sound of the nonstop rain dropping on the roof and the pavement, on the whole countryside.

"Yes," Somkit answered.

"Would you like to stay on?"

Somkit gave no answer. It should be plain to everyone after six weeks: uninvited and unrelated to the family, why would he stay on? He glanced at the host and then at Uncle K.

"Yes or no, just speak out. Don't act so shy, like a girl," the host said.

The word jabbed Somkit. Again he was alarmed that the comparison came so readily to grown-ups' lips, that they no longer saw him as a boy. He turned red.

Uncle K. merely smiled. "You decide." Egged on

by the host, Uncle K. seemed contented to stretch the visit into months.

Squinting, Mrs. Impeccable leaned forward and startled Somkit by grabbing his hand. "You can go fishing in the two fish ponds over there." She pointed with her left hand, her voice as coarse as her right hand, which still grabbed him. "Or go swimming in the reservoir. Treat it like a bath, soak in there."

Somkit stared through the gray misty rain: outside the house, the rectangular, brimful reservoir appeared like a giant bathtub in the open. He was in no mood for such amusements. He wished he could pull the stopper from Mrs. Impeccable's voice right now.

"You don't play enough," Mrs. Impeccable continued, still clutching his hand. "Why sit brooding by the stairs? Treat your time here as a vacation. You can play all day. Ride the water buffalo if you want." Just when Somkit thought she had finished, mischief returned to her eyes. She added, "Be like a boy," and winked.

At eight a.m. in the capital of Laos, the postal chief ambled into the rundown post office, whose architecture any person educated in the old system could pick out as French colonial. With hands behind his back, the chief passed his fellow Brothers, who, to start the day, had a sack of outgoing mail to inspect, but more likely to withhold. Letters to Canada, the U.S.A., Australia, France.

Seated at his desk, the chief marveled at the audacity of it—he even found some addressed to the refugee camps in Thailand. Did the people think he, overburdened by the volume of mail, would relax his guard? People from different parts of the country kept writing letters to overwork and distract him, just so out of all those fake letters they could slip the real ones, the treacherous ones, through.

Musing about the conspiracy against him, the chief rubbed his chin. He had decided to withhold all letters: with so many to inspect, his fellow Brothers would not trouble themselves to unseal the letters one by one with the steaming method.

Instead they tore them open. Because they could read none of the letters in French or Chinese, they turned them over to the language specialists.

One such letter, encrypted in Chinese, was written from a mother to her son; the address proclaimed Bangkok, Thailand, as its destination. After reading the letter, the specialist began the noble process of decoding, watchful for secret messages to freedom fighters in Thai provinces along the Mekong, alert for any reference to or symbolism of a call for arms, any collusion, any activities future and clandestine, any nuance of meaning at all, besides the literal meaning of a mother reminding the son to be patient and on good behavior, but mainly to be patient, for she would contact him soon.

At this point the stomach of the specialist made rumbling noises—time to eat. So he approved the letter, duplicated the handwriting of the addressee on an envelope, and let his footman seal it, drop it in the half-empty sack to be delivered onto the plane to Bangkok.

The letter arrived in Bangkok, where the patriotic

mailman turned the letters over to the chief inspector. All letters from the three neighbors—Cambodia, Laos, Vietnam—he detained for scrutiny. The chief inspector had his footman open the letter using a method known to only a few people in the world, an ancient Thai formula.

Inspectors versed in all Southeast Asian languages read the letters with a magnifying glass, searching for any messages hidden below the ink, any messages at all to the Communist rebels hiding in Thailand, any sign that would justify a crackdown. The police took pride in the result of the raids and the recent public burning of Communist propaganda—some printed in Vietnamese—in Sanam Luang, Bangkok.

The postmaster found a letter from Laos to the fourth sector of Bangkok. The penmanship on the envelope and in the letter didn't match. The dutiful citizen turned the missive over to the Thai police.

Without a return address, Somkit did not write to his parents. The use of the address in Bangkok would be hazardous, and writing about his new life in the countryside would alarm his parents. He suspected the Thais had withheld his parents' letters to him. If so, the Thais were keeping a watchful eye on Auntie K. and Big Brother. Had Auntie K. returned to Bangkok? There was no news of her.

No more letters from Laos.

Somkit sat by the stairs, staring at the distant, open rice field. When would his family come to get him? Six months later, or a year later, or ten years later, or never? But he couldn't sit idle, a mouth waiting to be fed. He had two options: he could either enter the refugee camp and wait to go to France, as Junda had done, or settle in Thailand, live under Auntie K.'s roof as a dependent, truly become Somkit, go to a Thai school, eventually become a Thai citizen. He stared at the distant, open rice field.

NIGHT

1995, San Francisco, California

"I returned to Bangkok after the political situation became stable."

Raymond asked Fong Mun if he satisfied his craving for cocoa.

Fong Mun admitted the diet was different, an answer that was not directly related to the question.

But Raymond sensed that Fong Mun, after returning to Bangkok from the countryside, had not satisfied his craving for cocoa. "Look at you. It's stunted your body."

Fong Mun's face turned ashen. His heartbeat quickened. The stunted, starved body that had been mistaken for being girlish . . . "Look at you, too." Fong Mun nudged Raymond's side with his elbow, to point out the difference in diet.

Raymond flashed a smile. "I grew up here. I drank plenty of milk."

"Flex your arms for me," Fong Mun teased, trying to recover.

Raymond flexed his right arm to show his biceps. Peeking out of his shirt's short sleeve, the dragon on his upper arm began to stir.

"That makes all the difference, doesn't it? Milk." Fong Mun sighed. "It made you grow into a strong, healthy young man." He moved his hand slowly along Raymond's arm. "You even have a tattoo. A dragon, huh?" His slow hand felt for the muscle. "Strong bone. Why don't you take off your shirt. Let me see how strong you are."

Raymond took off his shirt in one easy motion. He dropped it on the floor.

For a second Fong Mun's eyelashes fluttered: the dragon staring at him. Fong Mun stood up from the sofa and took a few steps toward the window.

How would Raymond see him? His skin had not yet dried with wrinkles, but he had love handles and a potbelly, the result of his trying to satisfy a phantom hunger which seemed to gnaw at his stomach incessantly. The remembered hunger—insatiable, vengeful—demanded him to make up for all the years of undereating. It kept tormenting him with pangs of emptiness until he could not help gobbling a mouthful. Love handles and a potbelly.

He couldn't care less how the world viewed him; he only cared how Raymond would see him. He had taken the risk and told Raymond how years ago people in Thailand mistook him for a girl. Raymond, who grew up without the notion of what a *katoy* was, who came from the land but was not of the land. Raymond, who grew up without either the burden of being labeled a *katoy* or the burden of the land. It followed that Raymond would not apply the ugly term to him. Even now, with eyes closed, Fong Mun could conjure up the look of disgust on Boontong's face, the kind that had conditioned him to turn against himself, to loathe himself for being gay.

In California, he had developed a healthier notion of himself. Being gay, his friend Tom had taught him, didn't mean being effeminate: "We can be well built, macho, and still have a straight woman's desire for a man." Listening to Tom, Fong Mun thought about such a desire trapped in a boylike, girllike body. He felt virile quite often, as when he worked in the garden, or when he exercised. He felt rugged. Yes, virility was as much a part of him as the delicacy that manifested itself in certain of his gestures, the way he prepared food, the language and tone of his cookbook.

"I intended to leave the countryside for Bangkok, to resist the host's hospitality."

"You were misunderstood," Raymond said.

Fong Mun turned his head slightly: I'm understood! He lowered his head. "I got used to the emptiness in the stomach, the void there. I began to think I didn't need to eat that much. The cocoa commercials only created the craving, enlarged the void."

The dragon took flight as Raymond stood up from the couch. "You were underfed without knowing it." Coming up behind him, Raymond put his hands on Fong Mun's shoulders.

Fong Mun tensed up, immobilized by the two magnetic opposites that coexisted in him, virility and delicacy, while the dragon, which now sprawled behind him, waited.

They faced the window. The overcast sky began to clear and the moon, vaguely visible, appeared as a round white plate above the bay. Still early to turn on the light.

"Condensed milk, cocoa, Ovaltine. So many brands of them. A luxury." Fong Mun crossed his arms. "I eventually left Bangkok and joined my family in the refugee camp. But the situation there got worse. I found out my mother had disappeared. According to my grandmother, it happened when my family crossed the border at night, in heavy downpour and thunder. They waited in the forest for the guide to lead them to the boat. My mother somehow got separated. No one knew what happened to her. They couldn't search and they couldn't go back."

A number of possibilities existed. Perhaps Mrs. Fong had fallen down in the dark, the mud being sticky or slippery, the heavy thunder and downpour drowning her cries for help. Perhaps she struggled to get to her feet and fell down again. Or the flood washed her away. Or, unable to find her way out of the forest, she developed a fever from being soaked by rain and fell into a delirium.

To risk missing the chance to cross the border, to delay the crossing, to look for the missing person, would jeopardize the efforts and safety of the group. They would get lost, or get caught, or get shot. He knew the route well and he would return to the forest at daybreak, the guide reassured Mr. Fong. The guide hurried the group into the boat. In the dark and the deafening rain, they failed to see the tumultuous billows of the river, how it swelled up. The river tossed the boat.

"My father now helps me tend to the garden in Sonoma County," Fong Mun said, as if trying to pull himself out of the past with this present-day information.

It made sense that after the boat reached the Thai border, the guide would sneak back to Laos the next day. But the river had risen so high and looked, in the daytime, so much more immense, so much more swollen, that the guide was compelled to hide in Thailand for a while until the river returned to calmness. And so the smuggler did not return to Laos the next day and make the urgent effort to search the route and the outlying area, or to find out if indeed the Brothers had caught Mrs. Fong. The third day, the sight of the rising river made the smuggler plead with Mr. Fong not to rush him. A month later, the smuggler, now hired by Mr. Fong, returned to Laos by the same route, but failed to find any clues in the forest with which he claimed to be so familiar. He went into the city and visited the prison. Did the Brothers release Mrs. Fong, or move her to a different location—or execute her? He asked around, used his contacts; but finding an answer was like looking for a needle sunk in the river.

To make peace with this uncertainty, the Fongs consoled themselves with this fiction: a villager had found the drenched, delirious, pneumonic Mrs. Fong, who never came to and was, a few days later, released from the cold hand of life. The villager would have pointed to a new grave in a clearing if the guide had managed to find him.

A hand gave Fong Mun's shoulder a firm squeeze. He turned and a hug seemed forthcoming—Raymond was ready—but Fong Mun was not to be consoled. He disengaged himself. It came that close, the possibility of contact, but he willfully—and selfishly?—spurned it. Renounced it. Trampled on it.

He walked to the sofa and bent over to pick up the shirt on the floor. As he reached for the shirt, he remembered the orange sweater his mother had knit for him. He still kept it, although it no longer fit him. He kept it in the suitcase, the same suitcase that he carried in his hand the day he left Luang Prabang. On that day, on the way to the jeep that would take him to the airport, he turned to look at his mother walking by his side, waiting for her to leave him some last-minute instructions, because he was leaving home for good. Instead, halfway to the jeep, she turned around and walked away from him, and he wondered how she could be so unemotional, her steps so resolute, as she headed indoors. Only years later did he understand her behavior. Feelings, he now learned, should be preserved, and not squandered through speech or any demonstrative outcry. To value feelings, then, he must not show or speak them, and to bear the intensity of feelings, he kept them under a surface of coldness. When he associated this surface coldness with that of his mother, he realized he had misunderstood her. As she headed steadily indoors, not turning back, what he saw now was not her heartlessness, but her strength. "Put it on, Raymond. Don't catch cold," he said, and slipped the shirt over Raymond's head.

Again Fong Mun turned to face the window. His arms folded, he watched the moon rise above the bay. "Shortly after my arrival in the camp, my grandmother got sick. She was making egg rolls in the kitchen when she fell down from a sharp pain in her leg."

1978, The Refugee Camp, Nongkhai, Thailand

The five-wheel pedal cab Mr. Fong summoned was parked by the roadside. While the cabman held the handlebars to steady the cab, Mr. Fong spread a cotton blanket on its bare aluminum seat. After he patted the blanket flat, he went inside the bamboo hut.

A moment later he and Ahma appeared at the door. He gripped her right arm while she, half a step at a time, limped from the door to the roadside. She jerked her right heel forward while dragging her left foot after. Halfway across the narrow gutter to the pedal cab, she paused and then slowly lifted her right leg. As it reached across the gutter, the right slipper dangled off her sole. Then with a jolt she tilted forward, groping the side of the pedal cab.

Unsure about what to do, Fong Mun stayed out of the way: he stood outside a next-door neighbor's hut, watching his father take Ahma to the pedal cab, his father's hands firmly clamped onto her arms.

Breathing hard through her mouth, Ahma paused by the edge of the pedal cab. After a second of rest she crawled onto the hard aluminum seat. She lay supine on the blanket and panted heavily. When the cabman started to pedal, she held onto the side, the March wind lifting strands of her white hair. A figure in a white blouse and a pair of loose black pants lying on her elbows in the pedal cab, gasping, she stared blankly into the ether. The cabman pedaled away.

Mr. Fong went indoors without seeing his son. A moment later Mr. Fong appeared at the door with a pillow and sheets bundled in his arms and hurried into the alley, again without seeing his son.

Fong Mun watched his father pass through the two rows of barracks along the alley. After his father turned left—where the alley merged with the main street—he returned indoors.

The Fongs' bedroom, on stilts, had a straw thatched roof and woven bamboo walls. Ahma had glued newspapers to the walls to seal off tiny apertures. In the makeshift kitchen, a piece of pork lay on the chopblock, next to the chopping knife. No shrimp or crab. The package of egg-roll wrappers—the hard, round rice sheet—lay unopened in the basket. The bean threads lay soaking in a bowl.

Fong Mun crouched down, picked up the knife, and started to chop. What to do with the meat and the rest of the material? He put down the knife and stood up.

* * *

He had never seen Ahma so ill. Her most severe illness had been a headache that lasted about ten days, and soon afterwards, in the morning, she was getting up before everyone else in the family. She even got up before the roosters and was already busy with chores when they woke up and started to crow, one after another.

Just as Fong Mun had hoped, Ahma returned from the hospital within a week. But she lay in the hut all day, all night. She never cooked again.

Ahma returned to the hospital soon after. This time the stay lasted two weeks or so. One late morning, Mr. Fong made a pot of plain porridge and put it in a canteen. Carrying the canteen, he then set out for the hospital with Fong Mun. The hospital was in the one-story timber administration building in the front of the camp. The camp, on the outskirts of Nongkhai province, was rectangular, enclosed on all sides by barbed-wire fence, with rows of barracks perpendicular to the two lengths.

In the ward, Mr. Fong put the canteen on the tiny stand next to Ahma's bed. He opened the canteen and asked if Ahma felt like eating porridge. She said she did not feel hungry. Fong Mun peered at the porridge—watery white, lukewarm, sticky—in the canteen. No scrambled egg, no salted fish. He himself did not even want to look at it twice, let alone eat it. It made sense that Ahma did not feel hungry. Mr. Fong left the porridge on the table. At the door, he turned around and asked Fong Mun to follow him outside.

In the sun, by the roadside, Mr. Fong reached into

his pants pocket and took out some money. Fong Mun
watched his father, who told him to use the money for
meals. To buy whatever he felt like eating for lunch
and dinner—and eat breakfast, too—but not to buy
Pepsi. Plain chemical stuff, those carbonated bubbles
had no nutritional value. Not good to skip meals and
be so pale and scrawny. Fong Mun lowered his head:
his hands looked like a pair of sticks that could be
easily snapped. His father pressed the money into his
hand. He watched his father walk off.

A few days later, Ahma was discharged again.
Back in the bedroom, lying on the cotton mattress, she
complained about the pain in her legs. She shifted to
lie on her side. Then, groaning, she shifted to the other
side. She asked Fong Mun to buy her a pack of mosquito coils because she had used up the last one.

A foot away from the mattress, he sat in the lotus
position on the bamboo floor. "I don't want to go," he
grouched. It was a hot afternoon in May, and the heat
made him irritable.

She pointed at the heap of ashes under the mosquito coil holder by her feet.

"Why don't you go get it yourself," he blurted
out.

She eyed him, then groaned. "Go buy mosquito
coils for Ahma," she asked again, feebly. A mosquito
flew from a corner and landed on the wall, its eyes
turning.

A few days later Mr. Fong again put Ahma in a
five-wheeled pedal cab. The cab bumped along the
dusty road. The cabman rang the bell as he made a

right turn. The pedestrians turned their heads as the cab passed by them. A figure in an unwashed Vietnamese outfit lying in the blanketed aluminum seat, white hair uncombed, Ahma stared blankly into the sky.

Fong Mun waited for Ahma's recovery. Two weeks passed. Then a month. The doctor transferred her to a new ward at the back of the hospital, a new one-story building with wooden walls, a cement floor, and a corrugated tin roof. The fifth week drew to a close, still no sign of recovery. The patient next to her left. A new one arrived, took up the bed next to her, and after a few days also left.

Oftentimes a group of refugees from the highlands of Laos arrived. These Hmongs had walked all the way—for weeks, and in most cases months—from their home in the mountains to the Mekong River. They swam across the border. After they reached Thailand, the Thai coast guards sent them in groups to the hospital in the refugee camp. The trek across the mountains had made their legs swell, thick as an elephant's. Their clothes became rags, their skin and hair sticky with dirt. Flies flew about them, grouped around their sores, gnawed at pus openings, while they kept their eyes closed. The Hmongs slouched on the floor along the wall, in between beds, because there were not enough beds. But even these hill-tribe people in time got well enough to leave.

Fong Mun began to get used to the thought that Ahma would have to stay in the hospital as long as the pain in her legs persisted. He saw months ahead and failed to project the day she would get out, and he remembered with shame what he had said to her one afternoon, how he had refused to buy mosquito coils.

Mr. Fong worked out a meal plan with the next-door neighbor. Fong Mun and his father would eat at the neighbor's place. Eating there made Fong Mun feel like a guest. As such, he was at the mercy of the host. The host—in this case, the housewife—could choose what and how much to cook, pull a long face at the dining table, or simply declare the lack of food and not serve anything at all. Fong Mun stood on ceremony, careful if he should eat too much and not leave enough for the neighbor kids, who stared at him as if he were a leech sucking their blood. Fong Mun knew his father had paid for their seats at the dining table, and he ate with some ease with his father seated next to him.

Feeling like a guest made him humble. And wordless. No doubt his silence created a tension for the neighbor's family. The meal plan turned into an awkward business deal, and eating a labor, so that the alternative seemed liberating: Fong Mun began to skip meals. He found freedom wandering around the camp at mealtimes. He got more and more used to the emptiness in the stomach. It produced a calming effect.

He also took to going to the hospital. He went there every morning. He sat by the window next to Ahma's bed, near the restroom. At ten he went to his English language class. After lunch he returned to the hospital and stayed until three or four. With the sun shining so high, parching everything in its presence, it was not so bad to spend hours inside the ward. He studied while Ahma slept. After she woke up, he asked her if she needed anything, whether she was hungry or thirsty.

Mr. Fong brought clothing and some porridge. When she saw the plain porridge in the canteen on the stand, Ahma turned away from it to face the wall (the restroom, in fact), without giving her son, who stood at the end of the bed, so much as a look.

"Why don't you eat, Ahma?" Fong Mun sat down in a chair by the bed.

"Ahma's not hungry." She still faced the wall.

Fong Mun leaned closer to her. "Do you feel like eating *mien* instead?" She grunted. "I'll get you a bowl of noodles," he added.

After a moment, she said no.

Fong Mun cast a glance at his father. His father said nothing. The hill-tribe patients lay along the wall. Mr. Fong spoke to Fong Mun. "What are you doing here, breathing in the stench? So unhealthful." He ordered Fong Mun to leave.

Fong Mun got to his feet, passed the restroom, and went outside. He stayed nearby, strolling back and forth along the strip of the road, and soon saw his father, carrying the canteen, leaving the hospital. After Mr. Fong went into an alley, Fong Mun returned to the ward.

A Hmong was at Ahma's bedside. The woman leaned near Ahma and spoke to her in a low, even voice. As Fong Mun stepped in, the woman stopped whispering and left Ahma's bed and returned to her group.

Fong Mun cast a glance at the group lying around on the floor against the wall. He turned to Ahma. "What was she doing here?"

"We know each other."

Fong Mun watched Ahma.

"She used to bring capons to sell to us, in Luang Prabang," Ahma said.

"It happened so long ago. Could be any Hmong."

"She remembers Ahma," Ahma said.

Fong Mun turned around. The woman already lay asleep, her feet drawn up. Haggard, worn out, thin. He tried to recall if he had seen her before. Could she be the vendor who, before the New Year, had unloaded cages of capons and bundles of firewood outside their home the photo shop? Or was she one of the hill-tribe customers Ahma had glared at because she found them so annoying? Fong Mun asked, "Ahma remember her?"

"If she said she used to sell us capons, then it must be true."

On a rainy night a Filipino doctor from the Red Cross came with a Thai doctor to Ahma's bedside. That night Ahma was the only patient in the ward. The two rows of beds along the walls lay empty. The Hmongs had gone.

The Filipino doctor took a look at Ahma, checked the IV bag, turned to the Thai doctor beside her and said something to him, and while they talked, Mr.

Fong stood by, in need of a translator, and the rain spluttered so loudly on the corrugated tin roof that the doctors had to leave the ward to talk in the lobby. Mr. Fong followed them into the lobby.

By the bedside Fong Mun watched—past the two rows of empty beds—the doctors talking to his father in the passageway. Did his father understand them? Did his father miss the details crucial to the status of Ahma's health?

The injections Ahma had every night seemed like thin icicles sinking down the river. The IV bag hung by the bed, with a tube and a needle in her arm. The needle marks in her arms, right and left, looked like bruises. Fong Mun lowered his head. He should have gone to buy her a pack of mosquito coils that afternoon. He didn't know what ailed her. He only knew Ahma had this pain in her legs all the time— sometimes, at night, she gasped till dawn.

On an overcast morning Fong Mun unlatched the barbed-wire gate to the ward, entered the courtyard, and saw, through the window, his father and Uncle Hahn talking in the lobby. The Hahns had been in the camp for nearly a year and a half and were still waiting to emigrate to France or Canada. Fong Mun was about to step in when he heard his father's voice. As he listened, his heartbeats quickened. He wished he had not heard them. He stole away.

Because of the rain, the roads had turned muddy and sticky and slippery, filled with puddles. He trudged cautiously on the main street, but each step made his slippers flip against his soles and slap some mud up his legs. No use trying to avoid getting soiled. No use.

He couldn't believe his father would think of sending him away again. To go to the United States by himself. They had had two interviews already and were now waiting for their names to appear on the departure list. In the ward, Mr. Fong had told Uncle Hahn that if their turn came up he would stay to care for Ahma. "Let the boy leave first."

Fong Mun went to a roadside stand to get a bowl of chicken noodles. The vendor had put up a tent. Dark clouds pressed low. The rice noodles were thick and short, sticky. The soup itself, also thick and starchy, was served with chopped cilantro, some fried chili paste, and black pepper. Fong Mun wished the vendor would give him, a regular customer, more chicken instead of the starchy soup with two or three cubes of coagulated pig blood. What chicken he got was all skin and bones. Usually he could eat three bowls of this. This time the prospect of again being sent away weighed on his mind. Dark clouds pressed lower. He soon finished sucking the last bone for flavor, still hungry.

After breakfast he returned to the hospital. As he trudged through the muddy main street, five-wheel pedal cabs rang their bells loudly and passed by him and other pedestrians. The cabs left tracks on the mud. Fong Mun trudged on.

Ahead of him, in the distance, a few buses were parked along the curb in front of the administration building, where a large throng of Hmongs gathered.

The buses would take them to Bangkok, where they would board the plane to resettle in far corners of the globe—in the United States, Argentina, parts of Europe—away from their homeland.

The Hmongs gathered outside the buses, below the bus windows, and sobbed. Those inside the buses, too, sobbed, reaching out their hands to hold onto the hands of those outside the bus windows.

A strong wind began to rise.

The drivers started the engines. The first bus, its roof loaded with the Hmongs' personal effects, began to drive off. The crying and talking grew louder, more frantic. The wind grew stronger, blustering. Hands let go of hands. Heads in the departing bus looked back, toward the camp, toward those left behind.

Watching the scene, Fong Mun then turned right and headed toward the hospital. The cloudy sky pressed lower. One day he would ride one of the departing buses.

When he came in, Ahma told him she had fallen down in the restroom. "How did it happen?" he gaped. "In the dark," she said. After a pause she added, "Ahma was a bit careless." Unable to get up, she had to crawl to her bed, dragging the IV bag along, wetting and staining her clothes. Did she change them? She uncovered a corner of the blanket: the needle had come off, the IV bag lay toppled by her knees.

Mr. Fong stepped in. Although earlier he had been in the lobby with Uncle Hahn, Mr. Fong had not come to Ahma's bedside, for when he found out what Ahma did, he raised his voice. "Do you have to get up in the

210

middle of the night? Do you?" She was too weak to answer him. He held her up by her shoulders, and as she leaned on his arms he unbuttoned her blouse. Fong Mun got up from the chair and went outside.

Ahma fell down many times. One day, as he took her to the restroom, Fong Mun tried to hold the bag over his head so as not to disturb the needle, while she hung on to him, her arm around his neck, and jerked her way there. At the door he handed the bag over to her to let her go in. As he waited by the door, he heard a plop. He turned around. Near the toilet bowl, Ahma was trying to get up from the floor, groping the wall, the IV bag dangling down her arm. He couldn't tell if the needle had come off. All he felt was bones as he helped her up. She hung on to him as he half-dragged her back to bed. She lay down, and gasped, and stayed in bed with her wet clothes on, her head turned to the wall. By this time he wished she would die quickly.

Later on Mr. Fong placed a container under Ahma's pelvis.

On a morning Mr. Fong came in to empty the container and change Ahma's clothes. She kept her eyes closed as he pulled the container from under the blanket. In the container was a dark red mess. A stench reeked from the bed. Mr. Fong turned around and looked at Fong Mun with stern eyes. "Why stand there? Go outside!" Fong Mun left the ward.

He walked quickly on the main street toward the market and did not slow down until he worked himself into a slight panting and sweating. Just then he stopped. Ahead of him, by the roadside, was Boontong. Fong Mun stopped under an awning of a coffee-house and watched the former revolutionary, once again, clad only in shorts.

Fong Mun had seen Boontong a few times in the camp, where familiar faces could be found: neighbors from Luang Prabang, family friends like Mr. Hahn, and faces that were neither intimate nor strange, like that of the shirtless revolutionary.

Boontong unloaded the block of ice from the five-wheel pedal cab parked on the road outside his ice distribution stall, a makeshift enclosure like a pigsty. As he lifted the thick flax cover off the block of ice, one foot wide, seven feet long, and one foot thick, it gave off vapor. Clusters of clouds were visible in the glistening glass brick.

Standing at the rear of the cab, Boontong clamped the block of ice with a pair of tongs and dragged it down a slide made of two planks of wood into the stall. He threw the tongs aside and stood wide-legged, his chest heaving.

When he sawed the ice, ice chips sparked and landed on the ground, on the flax cover, and on his suntanned arms, his hair, and melted. An ice chip jumped into his eye and it became glass for a second, before he blinked.

He used the tongs to clamp the chunk that he had just sawed and sank it in a tank of water made from the cross-sectional half of a gasoline tank. As soon as he sank it—just enough water to cover the ice—he lifted it and dropped it in a rectangular trough next to the tank. He then chopped the chunk to smaller pieces with a heavy cleaver.

As he chopped, sparks of ice chips caught his chapped hands and the wide legs of his boxer shorts and melted into them. Some sparks flew so high as to land on the nape of his neck, thrilling him.

He turned on a box-sized grinder and fed the chopped chunks to it; it rattled as the ice hit against the sides, was broken down, filtered through, dropped into the trough, and piled into a mound.

Boontong shoveled away the ice into two cylindrical ice chests. Then he put away the gear, lifted the ice chests onto the pedal cab, to get ready for delivery.

Fong Mun watched the bare-chested entrepreneur pedal off to distribute ice.

Ahma slept almost all the time. Her eyes closed, her cheeks sucked in, her mouth open: a dried specimen. When she spoke, or tried to, her mouth moved, mouthing soundless words, her eyes looking and not looking at anything.

Fong Mun could not make out what she said. Her hand raised. "I can't hear you," he said. "Louder, a little louder." Her hand dropped. He leaned forward, his ear tilted against her mouth: a wisp of dry air hissed from within. He finally understood. "Pepsi? No, no, Ahma, you can't drink that stuff when you're sick." He would not go buy a bottle for her.

Later in the afternoon, he found an empty Pepsi bottle on the windowsill. So his father, who forbade him to drink that kind of "chemical stuff," had bought it for her, a person so sick in bed. She had drunk it all.

She lost consciousness, or simply kept sleeping. The dark red mess kept showing up in the container.

Fong Mun had already stepped inside the hospital gate when he halted and looked through the open door into the ward. Three figures in long gray robes down to their ankles, their heads shaved, sat reading the sutra around Ahma's bed, a candle flickering on the windowsill. Dusk filled the ward. Where did the nuns come from, and who had asked them to come? He walked away quickly.

A few days later, he went to the hospital around nine in the morning as usual. Ahma was sleeping, her mouth agape. As he came near her, two or three ants darted onto her cheek and around her open mouth. He held two fingers under her nose and felt for her breath. He withdrew his hand but then tried again. He left the ward immediately and calmly returned to the hut.

He stayed in the bedroom, calmly sat leaning on the wall, calmly waited for his father, and calmly wondered if he was guilty of walking away and neglecting his duty, and if he was expected to emote in front of family friends and neighbors, instead of keeping a surface coldness, so composed. After an hour or so he couldn't contain himself any longer; he decided to return to the hospital. Yet the prospect of being alone with Ahma lying there still untended unnerved him. Perhaps by this time his father, or the nurse, had already discovered her condition. He returned to the hospital.

He didn't know what he felt—maybe disappointment—when he saw his father, together with Uncle Hahn, wrapping Ahma with a large sheet of white cloth. His father wrapped it around and around her into a rigid bundle while Uncle Hahn, holding her shoulders, kept her raised from the bed. A coffin lay open on the floor. So his father had already made preparations. He stood in the lobby by the window, watching them, but stole away before they could see him.

There was no pointed arch for an entrance to the temple, no swimming dragon to adorn each edge of the tile roof. Instead the temple roof was corrugated tin. The three walls stood waist-high, made of woven bamboo mats, so that the inside was visible from the outside. A dais for the monks to hold ceremonies adjoined the fourth wall. Grass mats covered the cement floor.

The Hahns and a few other family friends, those from the old hometown, showed up at the wake. On their knees, they moved across the grass mat toward the altar; each person lighted three joss sticks, shook the sticks to put out the flare at the tips, clasped the incense between fingers, turned to face the palm-sized black-and-white photo of Ahma on the coffin, brought the incense—the tips glowing red—toward their bosoms, bowed, and stuck the smoky incense in the container in front of the coffin. Watching this scene, even the living began to wish they were the dead, just to experience a rare moment of respect, dignity, and peace.

The visitors grouped around the coffin, and as they began to chat in low voices, found themselves oddly overcome by a sense of warmth and delight: so many familiar faces gathered in one place. Just like the New Year celebration in 1973, it occurred to them, the celebration in which the community gathered under one roof. Their last. Since then New Year's had become less intimate and more funereal, increasingly characterized by longings, solitude, absence of familiar faces, presence of shadows.

The visitors knew they should respect the occasion, which required them to look solemn and grief-stricken. They should, in keeping with their sense of propriety, at least try to keep their voices and facial expressions from becoming more and more animated. They should let their eyelids droop, eyes redden, instead of brightening.

The wake now partook of the spirit of the old New Year celebration for these refugees. The presence of familiar faces gathered under one roof—although around the coffin—was a comfort by itself. Sitting close together perhaps for the last time, wives asked after each other's well-being, husbands made small talk.

At eleven, Mr. Fong beckoned to Fong Mun, who sat next to the coffin listening to uncles and aunts chat about life in the old hometown. Mr. Fong told Fong Mun to return to the hut. Fong Mun said he didn't feel sleepy. Uncle Hahn too urged him to go back to the hut. Fong Mun glanced at the coffin mournfully and, next, at the uncles and aunts socializing. His eyes then lingered from the warm, soothing sociable scene back to the black-and-white photo of Ahma on the coffin, the lone candle burning next to the canister of incense. The candle wax the only tears shed for the dead. Some more joss sticks needed to be added. Fong Mun turned to face the two seniors. He could stay awake, he said. But the seniors again sent him away. He turned his back.

Under the starry sky, he walked on a side street that merged with the main street, which circled an empty, dusty field, the heart of the refugee camp. All dark now, because the electrical power in the camp had gone off. All the buildings, or rows of barracks, rather, each separated by an alley, converged on the main street. Shuffling along the main street, Fong Mun passed the shops, passed Boontong's ice distribution stall, turned left into an alley. The residential units in the two rows of barracks along the alley were all dark. No flickering candle, no lighted oil lamp, no red cigarette tips in sight. Fong Mun reached the end of the alley, where the hut stood. Some laughter and voices from the opposite hut were audible. On and off, the neighbors there still provided meals for the Fongs.

Outside the door, Fong Mun took a deep breath and a look at the starry sky, before he lifted the bar and stepped in. The door opened with a *"cork . . ."* sound, the way tall bamboo trunks swung at night, in the grove. He didn't want to hear any noise, or wish to make any. He moved, his steps light, toward the room, unlatched another door.

The bamboo mat creaked as he moved around: lighting a candle, changing clothes, folding his white shirt and the pair of grayish yellow pants to wear for the funeral. The pants were wrinkled from his kneeling all night. He spread the mosquito net, hooked it, then lifted a corner of it, ducked inside, covered himself with a blanket. Lying down, he heard voices, light voices, from neighbors in the opposite hut.

Two trucks made up the procession. The one with the coffin in it led the way through the main street. The other truck followed, filled with seated townspeople, some uncles and aunts from the Fongs' hometown, among them the Hahns, and several unknown faces— the Laotian elders.

Fong Mun knelt by the coffin and tried to fix his attention on the running engine, conscious that people were peeking from the shops as the procession moved past. His nose caught some sort of odor, maybe balm or oil.

He should be crying. He recalled a typical scene in movies: the family kneeling around the coffin, the widow howling—her cries penetrating the sky— pounding her chest, tearing her hair. Then she passed out. The siblings, heads down, eyes watery red, sobbed quietly. Banners with large black words flapped in the wind. The widow, as soon as she revived, rushed forth to dash her head on the coffin, but her children held her back, their hands clutching her shoulders.

Fong Mun felt odd because his eyes were dry. He peered at his father by the coffin: his father's eyes, too, were dry. And none of the uncles and aunts, none of the family friends, cried—except Uncle Hahn. He wept copiously by the coffin, wetting his sleeves, his eyes bloodshot and thick lips shaking.

Uncle Hahn had known Ahma all his life, the woman with the formidable voice. They had lived in Hanoi, adopted the Vietnamese customs and language, and when they fled to Laos and settled in the capital and Luang Prabang, also adopted the Lao customs and language. Uncle Hahn wept.

The procession passed the hospital and the administration building on its way toward the sentry post. At the checkpoint a Thai sentry lifted the bar to let the trucks through, unchecked.

Newly arrived in Laos, Uncle Hahn had decided to stay in the capital, while the Fongs, mother and son, chose a different path. And so the Green Fishtail joined the procession of newcomers, taking the Fongs over the mountains and passing the highlands that in later years were beset by guerrillas. Accompanied by the flock of birds and butterflies, the newcomers drove from the capital through the new country, an unknown terrain, to the home of the Golden Buddha, Prabang. Years later, after he married, Mr. Fong locked up the Green Fishtail in the garage.

Once outside the refugee camp, on the highway, the trucks ran smoothly, not too fast or too slow. The coffin bumped.

Back in Luang Prabang, funeral processions lasted

longer. Sheets of white cloths covered the whole truck. Relatives and community leaders carried white flags with large black words of condolence and marched all the way to the cemetery, each step heavy with solemnity.

In no time the trucks turned off the highway to a gravel road that led to a Thai temple, and stopped outside the entrance. Fong Mun followed the people through the pointed arch, across the lawn, and to the temple, where sunlight could not get in and where statues of Buddha retained the serenity of stone inside a cave.

Mr. Fong was not among those stepping across the threshold into the cavelike interior. The coffin was not carried in. Fong Mun followed the people inside, and when they knelt down in front of the Buddha in the center, he too knelt down. A few monks came in from a side door and sat in the lotus position in a row on the floor, which was covered with a dyed grass mat, in front of the Buddha. The ceremony began. Fong Mun lowered his head until the monks' chanting stopped. Then the people rose to leave. He stood up, too, and followed them outside.

He stood among the spectators gathered by the steps of the temple. They had no idea he was the grandson of the woman whose body now lay in the crematorium. From their vantage point, the crematorium was a cylindrical building several stories high, looming on the far right side of the temple. Centuries ago Lao warriors might have used it as a lookout tower to spot the Siamese enemies riding on elephants across the plain. At the top, the coffin lay in front of the furnace.

A monk pushed the coffin in. The fire spilled from the mouth of the furnace, tips leaping from the deep orange glow within. Fong Mun wondered if Ahma was really in that pile of fire, her body sizzling, scorched, reduced to bones. He wondered how long it took. For the fire to burn like this, the body had to be soaked with oil, cans of it on the clothes of the dead, on her shoes. Some coursed into her ears, tracing the grooves. The leaping shadows on the furnace stilled themselves, gradually faded. Smoke expelled from the chimney.

"Time to leave," someone below the steps announced.

Fong Mun followed the crowd through the lawn, out the pointed arch, and got on the truck parked on the road. No one stayed. Fong Mun looked about him: his father was not in the truck.

The funeral attendees sitting around Fong Mun were strangers, not the uncles and aunts he had known. Surely they didn't know Ahma? They didn't even know what she looked like. They would probably picture her as a woman in a sarong, her teeth blackened from having chewed beetle nuts all her life, rather than a Chinese in a Vietnamese outfit yelling at customers in Laotian. But they were Buddhists who had fled their homeland to the refugee camp: they attended the funeral to practice kindness.

On the highway Fong Mun looked through the truck window. In the distance a ladder of smoke leaned diagonally into heaven, over the open rice field. The trucks ran at full speed.

Fifteen minutes later Fong Mun was back in the camp, shuffling in the alley to the hut. He entered the hut. In the bedroom he slumped on the floor and leaned on the wall. When he heard ticking, he peered at Ahma's round clock in the corner: barely mid-afternoon. Next to the clock was the round string of the prayer beads.

The departure was abrupt, leaving the ashes, or bones, still in the furnace, not knowing what would happen to them. Who would put them in an urn? A novice monk? How could he tell the ashes from the wood? What if he spilled some on the ground? Suppose he overlooked a portion of the ashes, or pieces of small bones?

The clock ticked. Fong Mun fumbled in the pocket of his trousers and took out some coins. He had half a baht. He changed into a pair of shorts, locked the door, and shuffled toward the market. Ahead of him, Boontong was working in the ice stall. Fong Mun walked up the stall. He took a deep breath and went in. "I want to buy some ice," he said.

Boontong turned around.

The fleeting eye contact told Fong Mun that Boontong recognized him. Did he appear girlish, with his messy thick long hair that touched his eyes, yet with his Adam's apple showing?

Boontong looked away. "How much?" A layer of shaved ice on his eyebrows.

Was he such a repulsive sissy? Fong Mun extended his hand.

Boontong glanced at the coins in Fong Mun's palm and turned toward the cylindrical ice chest. He took out a small plastic bag from a stack hooked to the post and filled it with some ice from the ice chest. Doggedly refusing eye contact, he handed the ice bag to Fong Mun.

Tears burst from Fong Mun's eyes. He pushed the bag away and rushed out. The coins dropped to the floor.

At night, Fong Mun cried again. He felt obliged to and he felt sad. As he thought of crying, tears came.

A few days later Mr. Fong said he would take Fong Mun to see the tomb after it was built. From what Fong Mun heard after the funeral, he gathered that Ahma died of cancer. He didn't know what kind: he never asked his father, and his father never told him.

The crematorium stood still in an early November afternoon. The temple, the stupa, and the lawn with short dry grass, too, stood still. No monk appeared in sight.

Mr. Fong, in his white shirt and gray pleated pants, shuffled along the length of the white-plastered temple wall, his sandals kicking up the dust. Fong Mun followed him. When his father stopped, Fong Mun stopped too. His eyes caught Ahma's palm-sized black-and-white photo on the wall. The greased white hair just above the shoulder, the corduroy jacket she wore.

Not exactly a tomb, not what he thought it was. The monk must have placed the urn inside the wall.

His father looked pleased, proud of Ahma's resting place, and bent down to scrape away the leaves fallen in front of the tomb.

Fong Mun had thought Ahma would have a tomb of her own, instead of occupying a part of the temple wall in a foreign land. Back in the old home, Ahma would have been buried in the community cemetery. Fong Mun himself would have worn a square inch of black cloth on his shirt sleeve for a hundred days, the mourning period. "What ceremony? What rituals?" Mr. Fong had said to family friends during the wake. "The present circumstances don't allow for our traditions."

Fong Mun went to see the "tomb" one or two more times before he left for America. The morning he left the camp, he turned around to take one more look as the bus passed the turnoff to the temple.

Raymond spoke, "You had no one else to cook for you."

"Ahma's biggest worry—no one to cook. She always feared that it would happen to us, hunger, personified by the Brothers. But . . ." Fong Mun sighed. "Once in the States, my father picked up the knife and the chopblock."

"Did he know how to cook?"

"It never occurred to me he would care to cook, until in the refugee camp when I saw the porridge he made for Ahma, his first awkward attempt. But in the U.S. he made stir-fried squids with bok choy."

"Your father must have recipes in his head," Raymond said.

"He saw Ahma cook all his life. He probably remembered more than I did. But when it comes to cooking, he lacks patience."

And then a voice interjected—Ahma: "Grandson,

your father simply lacks hands-on experience. He needs practice."

Another voice—Mr. Fong: "In Laos, when I saw him in the kitchen watching Ahma chop meat, I would order him to leave there at once and go play in the playground. I chased him out of the kitchen with the authority of my voice."

Ahma: "But when I saw him wallowing in the playground with Auntie K.'s boys, I would order him to go indoors at once and stay by my side in the kitchen. I chased him away from the playground with the authority of *my* voice." A sigh; her voice then became reflective and mournful: "For the boy's father, cooking becomes a burden fit for a maid or a wife. He's tired from work."

"Tired from work, maybe," Fong Mun grudgingly admitted. "His attitude is that the kitchen is not a man's territory."

Mrs. Fong: "Surely not his. He would rather eat out if he can afford it."

More voices now.

Mr. Fong: "I realized Fong Mun has to cook. He's been critical of my cooking from the very beginning. I don't see a way out. I too learned to cook from memory and I cook what I can. He either bears with me or learns to stoop down and cook for himself."

Ahma: "It's a necessity, a responsibility."

Mr. Fong: "This too I realize."

Mrs. Fong: "You realize all too late. Think about the price you paid to come to this realization."

Fong Mun: "Even in Bangkok I merely helped

Auntie K. with the chores. I never actually cooked or decided what to cook."

Mr. Fong: "This may sound harsh, but you will have to in America if you don't want to starve."

The visitation of voices often came unannounced, rising and falling, making Fong Mun's head their center stage, a spinning vortex, their unbounded centrifuge.

1980, San Francisco, California

Whenever Mr. Fong cooked, smoke would fill the whole apartment. Father and son had just moved out of an acquaintance's apartment in Oakland to a public housing unit in San Francisco. As soon as they moved in, Mr. Fong removed the smoke alarm from the kitchen. When he cooked, he opened the windows and the door, turned on the fan. Even so, the smoke would cling to the clothes of the father and son and cling, too, to the cartons of lettuce and garlic that the son tried to grow on the windowsill.

If a fish sizzled in the pan, the two inhabitants would catch the smell of fish on them. The fish stink crept into their clothes, their hair, and even onto their skin—a smell worse than that of burned food.

But Mr. Fong's nose, sniffing, couldn't tell the difference. He worked in the fish and meat section of a grocery store. He smelled and handled fish all day long. The fish smell took up residence in his fingernails, in the grooves of his ears, in his scalp. He brought the smell to the apartment and turned the place into a phantom fish market: the stink permeated, but not a fish to be found.

One evening, he prepared the cheapest of all seafood—squid. He used a small knife to make gridlike patterns on them before cutting them to strips. The patterns would turn the squid simmering in the wok into pieces of miniature sculpture; their heads and tentacles made up a wild blossom.

Fong Mun had seen Ahma cook squid this way.

Mr. Fong added oil to the pan and, when it heated up, added some garlic that he'd smashed with the back of a chopping knife. When the garlic turned golden, he threw in the squids and stirred them quickly. They sizzled, turned purplish, curled into pieces of sculpture. He threw in the bok choy, stirred, covered the pan. As the contents simmered, he mixed a spoon of cornstarch with half a bowl of water, then added some fish sauce to it. When the bok choy was cooked, he poured in the bowl of watery cornstarch. He stirred the mixture. The liquid part of it thickened. He moved the contents to a plate. When left in the pan too long, they would become too starchy, the liquid too thick. He quickly added some black pepper.

He learned it from Ahma, Fong Mun thought as he observed his father. Mr. Fong again smashed the garlic cloves with the back of the knife and unwrapped the butter. He added butter to the same pan, without washing it, and turned on the heat, and threw in the garlic, and as the garlic sizzled, he quickly added a slice of beef, copying the way Ahma made steak in their old home.

"Come wash hands. Time to eat," the chef commanded as he transferred the steak from the pan to a plate. He added some butter and garlic and another slice of beef to the pan.

Fong Mun dried his hands on a towel and sat down. Even with the windows open and the fan on, his clothes and hair already stank of fried garlic.

The squids were cut too big, he thought, as he chewed tentatively, testing. Too salty.

"Eat the steak," his father reminded him, and took up a knife and fork to cut it. The cutting turned up meat still raw. Each cut pushed more blood out. His father put a piece of red meat in Fong Mun's bowl.

He protested, "No, no," and picked it up with the chopsticks and dropped it back on the plate. A pool of watery blood oozed through the steak. He turned his eyes from it to his father.

"Raw what? This is called nutrition." His father picked up the piece with his chopsticks and put it back in Fong Mun's bowl.

"There's still blood in it. Look." He showed his father.

Mr. Fong glowered.

Fong Mun sensed the contempt that showed up in the corner of his father's eye. He stiffened. If he were more of a male, he would eat that steak. Only a sissy would fuss with his father over a piece of red meat. Any straight male would have gladly chewed it, swallowed it, converted it to machismo.

People, now in the States, had not made the mistake others, in Thailand, had. He was no longer mistaken for a girl, although he still grew his hair long, almost shoulder-length. He wouldn't know how to talk to the haircutter in English—and he lacked the dollars.

He lifted his head and stared at his father.

His father wouldn't look him in the eye but used his voice instead. "I've told you to eat. Why don't you?" Fong Mun slapped the meat back in the plate. His father looked angrily at him. "It has to be cooked over," Fong Mun said. His father stood up, grunted, reheated the pan, flung in the piece of meat.

After dinner Mr. Fong used the hand towel to wipe the sink, and after wiping it he used the same towel to dry the dishes he had just washed.

"That towel is dirty," Fong Mun cried out.

"It doesn't matter."

"Doesn't matter? You've just used it to wipe the sink."

Mr. Fong wouldn't listen.

"The sink is dirty, the bowls are clean," Fong Mun repeated.

It made no difference.

Some distance away, the window of their neighbors' brightly lit kitchen was discernible from the Fongs' kitchen window. Many tenants in the neighborhood were Southeast Asian refugees. A middle-aged couple and two children gathered at their dining table for their lunar New Year's Eve dinner. In his unlit kitchen, Fong Mun could make out dishes and bowls on the table of his neighbors. The cold air must have magnified the ordinary fifty-watt light bulb in the neighbor's kitchen, for its warm glow filtered through the window into the cold and the dark. The cold air must have also amplified the sound, for Fong Mun could hear the clink of the spoons touching the china bowl.

His stomach growled.

He went downstairs to the parking lot. Then he went to the laundry room. He looked around the garage. Working overtime again? He pictured his father still hosing fish guts and scales off the floor, gathering them in a heap and throwing them in the garbage. A shrill wind blew past Fong Mun, making his night clothes and even his very body seem porous, causing sharp goosebumps to rise on his skin. He hurried indoors, and the dark, too, seemed to have crept in and couldn't be dispelled even with the light on.

He opened the refrigerator. He felt like eating the steamed ground meat that Ahma used to make. But he lacked the right ingredients. The easiest, quickest way would be to add two eggs to the ground pork, add some water, fish sauce, and black pepper, blend them well, shred a green onion into the mixture, pan-fry it. He took out a package of pork.

He squatted down with the chopblock and the package of pork. He laid the chopblock on the floor. He had started chopping meat when the kitchen door swung open and Ahma walked in.

She loomed over Fong Mun as he looked up. She asked him what he was making. He had no ready answer. Faltering, he told her he planned to steam the meat and eat it with rice. Downstairs neighbors would complain about the chopping, she said, already sounding like an American, for the idea of neighbors complaining was new to her. And to Fong Mun, too. She sat on the sofa, where she could see him hunched over to chop meat.

Ahma still wore the white blouse and the pair of wide-legged black silk pants. She had that haggard, starved look, as if no amount of food could ever restore her. Her eyes seemed the only live part of her. The wrinkled skin clung to her; her hair was thin, her hands and feet scrawny, her cheeks sucked in. Everything about her looked shriveled, but when Fong Mun looked at her, her eyes filled with tenderness.

Fong Mun became conscious of Ahma looking and of how he appeared to her—in his night clothes, stooped on the floor doing a maid's job. His face turned spicy hot, all the way to the roots of his ears. And his hunger made him angry. He hated to cook, not knowing how, making a spectacle of himself. Tears quickly gathered in his eyes. He looked away from Ahma, fixed his eyes on the chopblock.

Ahma had stopped talking and just sat there on the sofa. She sat for fifteen minutes and stepped out.

When Fong Mun looked up, Ahma had gone.

He took a deep breath. He added fish sauce to the ground pork and put it in the steamer. While he waited for the water in it to boil, he sulked, his anger reducing his hunger. By the time he sat down for dinner, he did not feel hungry anymore.

He chewed the food. The more he chewed, the

more he found it distasteful, like the porridge his father had made for Ahma.

His sight—the rice in his bowl and the steamed pork in the bigger bowl on the table—began to blur: all the colors in the world crowded in his eyes. As he blinked, huge tears dropped into his bowl. He slammed it on the table and covered his face with his hands, the tasteless mess stuck in his mouth.

Afterwards he wiped the spilled rice from the table and washed the dishes. He sat on the sofa, turned on the TV, sunk in the kind of mood that followed after a cry.

New Year. He had a yearning to see the headlights of cars coming toward him and the red taillights passing him, up and down the hilly streets. He grabbed a jacket, tied his sneakers.

He roamed on the cold dark streets, block after block. The wind shook the street sign. A car or two passed him. He looked into the cars. Anyone out there celebrating the New Year's Eve? Any family on the way home from their annual reunion dinner? Did they have homemade *jong?* Rice cooked in capon fat? The red taillights crowded his eyes. It began to drizzle. Something hot touched his face. It quickly became cold.

His shoes would get wet. The apartment would be quiet with chill, a funeral parlor, and the weak light-bulb would be better off than on. He had a number he could call, the number of a man named Tom, the businessman who had approached him on Van Ness during one of his roamings on a winter night.

He used a pay phone.

He entered the man's home about half an hour later. Tom asked him to remove his wet shoes. Shivering near the heater, Fong Mun removed his socks as well. Tom gave him a towel. While Fong Mun dried his feet with the towel, Tom sat down on the sofa. Rubbing the towel around his toes, Fong Mun asked if he knew tonight was the lunar New Year's Eve. Tom seemed absentminded, didn't respond to Fong Mun. Instead, Tom's hands began to move.

The purpose, the speed, and the urgency that accompanied the movement of the hands surprised Fong Mun. He moved closer to the heater. The pair of hands followed him.

The caresses struck Fong Mun as fake, excessive and theatrical: Tom's groans, his half-closed eyes. Did he know that tonight was the lunar New Year's Eve? Fong Mun burst into tears.

Tom looked up, shocked, his engrossing activity cut short. A trail of saliva flying from his mouth, Tom asked questions. Why did he call? Why did he come to his home?

Fong Mun blinked, and said he just wanted to drop by. Why did he come here, Tom asked again, more sharply this time. Fong Mun looked at Tom but said nothing. Tom's eyes turned angry. "You're not answering my question."

Fong Mun repeated, "I was on the street, and I thought why not go to your house, so I called you up."

"You're not answering my question." The man shook his head.

"I already told you. What else is there to say?" What else can be the reason for dropping by the house of someone you know, other than the act of dropping by because you want to? Fong Mun, now under pressure, fumbled for possible right answers, and knowing that people in America valued open communication (already Tom regarded him with suspicion), he forced himself to explain why, stuttering and muttering and wriggling his toes, and he ended up spilling something quite unintended—and, of course, unrelated to the core question.

"You tie the allegiance to your history with your choice of a lover? That's unfair."

"So?" Fong Mun brushed his hair to the right. He added that he felt bored now.

"Bored?" Wide-eyed and unblinking, Tom regarded Fong Mun with amazement.

Tired also of the theatricality of the man's response, Fong Mun answered in the affirmative, whereupon the man jumped to his feet. "You sure know how to make a guy feel good."

He asked Fong Mun to leave.

What? Fong Mun almost cried out. How can you be so final, so absolute? "My shoes are still wet." He pouted.

"All right. You can sleep on the sofa." Tom grunted.

*   *   *

The two developed a platonic friendship after the lunar New Year's Eve. Fong Mun came to see that New Year's Eve did not have the same meaning for other people as it did for him, and that New Year would continue to call to mind something irrevocable and mournful. This knowledge set him apart. It made him lonely. And when asked what he did for the New Year, he would mutter and stutter. And his answer—his English notwithstanding—would appear awkward, roundabout, slippery, a put-on, an outright lie, frustrating for those seeking an account of celebration.

Better to focus on something more upbeat, like starting a business.

He was determined to find a substitute for the hard rice sheets used as wrappers, naive enough to believe that he could find them. He did, eventually. In the freezer of a Southeast Asian grocery store. Two brands: one was labeled "egg roll"; the other, "multipurpose"—also used for *lumpia* and tortilla. He chose the one intended strictly for egg roll. It turned out to be the wrong choice: the wrapper, when chewed, became gummy and stuck to the teeth—exactly why he had decided to replace the rice sheets. Next, he decided to try the multipurpose wrapper, shuddering at the thought of his egg rolls turning into tortillas. He tried it anyway. It turned out to be the best choice, and he had used it ever since.

"It shouldn't take the whole afternoon to make thirty egg rolls," Tom said to Fong Mun. Tom broke down the whole process into individual steps and timed

Fong Mun to see how long he spent on each: shelling and deveining the prawns, mincing them, soaking the bean threads, cutting the wood ear and jicama, seasoning and mixing the ingredients in a large bowl, making the sauce, peeling the wrappers, wrapping, frying.

The result: "You spend too much time on shelling and mincing the prawns, and when you wrap, you tend to linger over the amount of stuffing in each," Tom said. "Don't try to decide if this one or that has too little prawn or too much bean thread. Just speed up. It should take less than a minute to wrap one."

He advised Fong Mun to predetermine the amount of stuffing. "Once you've decided on the amount, go ahead and wrap. Your hands should be unthinking. Once you finish wrapping one, get ready for the next. A wrapper should be ready to go."

The idea horrified Fong Mun. It jolted him from the reflections of childhood he indulged himself in while cooking. Fong Mun saw himself running in and out of the kitchen in his home in Laos. He saw Ahma chop pork, sort the crabmeat, devein the shrimp, soak bean threads, wet the hard rice sheets, peel the jicama, shred the wood ear, wash the green lettuce, crack eggs, season the mixture, wrap, heat the wok with firewood, fry, make the sauce. Now he wondered what occupied her mind as she went through the motions. She must have made egg rolls for the same reason he did.

"Keep the time spent on peeling the wrappers to the minimum." Tom cut into Fong Mun's reverie. "Every egg roll should have equal length and thickness. I'll time you."

Deferring to Tom's business acumen, Fong Mun cut down the time and became more efficient. He realized he had been too slow and sentimental while wrapping, taking too much time measuring, deciding, folding the egg roll, and if not satisfied, refolding it.

"Make the sauce in advance." Tom, always the rational accountant, came up with this idea: "Put in an equal amount of everything—an equal amount of water, sugar, fish sauce, and vinegar. So the sauce won't taste too sweet or salty or sour, because it has all three. All equally sweet, salty, and sour. Makes sense?"

Tom called Fong Mun's attention to the evenness of color of French fries. "A wok can't do that for you." So Fong Mun invested in a fryer.

Neither of them had counted on the amount of time it took to wash it. After Tom went home, Fong Mun cleaned up. He didn't have to time himself to know that the electrical contraption created more work than a wok did. To wash the fryer, he had to detach the strainer, plus its handle and the two lids. He had to detach the sealing lid to get to the bottom lid. The fryer came with a short electrical cord which could not be detached, so Fong Mun had to try to keep the cord dry when washing the clumsy five-pound contraption. Then he had to dry the parts and reassemble them. He found a short thin stick which he didn't know what to do with. He never used the fryer again.

She threw open the door of Fong Mun's memory and stepped in, with some rigidity in her manner. She led him through the steps without talking. He saw her hands clearly, how she steamed ground pork with the eggs she had blended and the bean threads she had soaked, how she made steamed spareribs in black bean sauce. After she went through the steps, she walked out the door.

Ahma: "Over time, he tries out other variations. Such as his version of green peas with prawns, simply because the pink-red color of the prawns and the bed of green peas complement each other and create rich visual appeal. He improvises. He substitutes green peas for green soybeans."

As Ahma walked through the door of Fong Mun's memory to offer cooking lessons, Fong Mun's mother lurked behind the door. One day she, too, would step through.

"And so cooking became a pleasure," said Raymond.

"Yes, and a means to entertain friends. And to impress you, I hope."

Raymond broke into a toothy grin. "You make the best egg rolls."

As he turned on the halogen lamp behind the sofa, Fong Mun thought for a second. After the voices quieted down, perhaps it was time to close his business. Perhaps any day soon he would delete the egg rolls from the catering menu.

Through the window, across the bay, the full moon lay half submerged in the passing clouds. "We're all guests." Fong Mun looked to Raymond. "Auntie K., her daughter Junda, Uncle Hahn, the Hmongs, the boy practicing martial art, my grandmother, myself, and even Boontong, the Blessed Copper—we're all guests, each in a host country that is our new garden. Uncle Hahn ended up in France, Junda in Australia, Ahma buried in Thailand. We moved from country to country, from garden to garden. We adopted different tongues, went by different names—picked up different recipes."

"And we end up here," Raymond muttered.

"The boy practicing martial art?" Fong Mun mumbled. "He must have gone to Thailand, and then to France or Canada." Fong Mun would never see him again, but saw him as a man—a lone figure—gaunt, adrift in the world, beyond retrieval. Even if he saw him, he wouldn't recognize him. In his head Fong Mun replayed the boy's stance, the way he positioned the pole in the middle of the medicine store. He savored the pleasure that the sudden sight of the boy's body had given him—the pleasure that would last a lifetime.

Fong Mun had kept some egg rolls in the refrigerator, but neither he nor Raymond felt ready for dinner.

Fong Mun's feet touched something that had just dropped on the floor—Raymond's shirt.

Now Fong Mun turned to Raymond. The dragon on Raymond's upper arm wriggled. Fong Mun moved his tongue along the body of the dragon. He closed his lips on the dragon's head, on its bulging eyes. The dragon curled around the tip of his tongue.

The moon was submerged in the bed of clouds. After they slipped past it, it became visible again, pale yellow, a gilt mirror. The sky seemed to have a crack, right by the moon, streaks of greenish light. A nebulous presence.

"That's the dragon," Fong Mun whispered, peering out the window. "An angry dragon. There, his claws. See the scratch? The streaks? The angry dragon in the sky, right above the city."

"Right above us," Raymond moaned as Fong Mun worked his tongue over the dragon.

"Impregnating the moon in front of heaven."

"Right before its very eyes."

"Ravishing the moon goddess."

Fong Mun brushed the sweat on Raymond's forehead, around his eyes. Beads of sweat on his nose tip, at the temples, around the curve of his ears, along his neck. His skin, his veins, his whole body, glimmered.

As Fong Mun closed his lips on the dragon, Raymond let out another moan, almost imperceptible. If Fong Mun had not happened to look up and see Raymond's Adam's apple going up a notch and quickly down, his lips parted, he would have missed it. Fong Mun inhaled breaths moist like musk. He closed his mouth on Raymond's throat.

Thunder.

He darted his tongue on Raymond's throat and he felt the movement of the cartilage up and down, the Adam's apple pulling his mouth along, up and down, it seemed.

They would heat up the egg rolls later.